Advance praise for
The Plague Confessor

"The title story, 'The Plague Confessor,' written before the current pandemic, showcases just how much society can change in a crisis, in both good and bad ways. The other stories that make up Smith's collection highlight dark glimpses into the underbelly of humanity, along with the poignant sense of loss and what it means to live."

-- Mary Hart, author, Some Horrific Evening

"Meg Smith's *The Plague Confessor* is a multifaceted gem that reflects times of a society in social distancing. It is a must-read.

- Jerry Langdon, editor, Raven Cage Zine

"*The Plague Confessor* is an addictive read, and a must for all fans of dark fiction. The stories in this collection are dark, twisted, and humorous in parts. You'll smile despite your uneasiness. These tales of mystery and imagination will send a chill down your spine more than once!"

-- Glynn Owen Barass, author and editor;
game writer, Call of Cthulhu

D1521207

Acknowledgements

This short story collection includes previously-published short stories, spanning 1993 to 2020.

Some of the short stories appear here in slightly different form, and with different titles.

The publications in which some of these short stories first appeared include *Into the Darkness, The Blue Lady, Raven Cage Zine, Outer Darkness, The Creativity Webzine, Dark Dossier, The Sirens Call eZine,* and *Heliocentric Net.*

Book layout and design: Eric Stanway.

Cover photo by Adam Duclos.
From "Restless Dreams," performed to Disturbed's recording of "Sounds of Silence" by Simon and Garfunkel. Performed at Danse Macabre, Tribal Bellydance Troupe Eve's 10th anniversary showcase. New Players Guild Theatre, Fitchburg, Mass., Nov. 19, 2016.

The Plague Confessor

[handwritten inscription: Lowell Folk Festival 7/27/2024 To Jan, In the spirit of ...]

Meg Smith

Emu Books

Contents

Author's Introduction

Photo credit: Meg Smith
The author's professional photo, with improvised face-covering.

As I finish this book, my first collection of short stories, the world is convulsing with a disease of mysterious origins, a place whose exact location remains disputed.

All we know for certain is that — COVID-19 — the illness borne of the family, coronavirus — has gripped the planet, and its cost in life, and livelihood, is high.

Talk of "getting through it," while perhaps uplifting, strikes me as disingenuous. The people who have died, and their families and loved ones, are not "getting through it," as though merely watching a scary movie or TV series.

It is a true pandemic, and as pandemics are wont to do, it has many people indoors, away from others, and seeking some solace.

For me, writing has always provided a means of solace.

Photo credit: Meg Smith

Dressing as a witch for a birthday parade. Parades became popular during the coronavirus crisis, when celebratory gatherings were restricted.

The impact of the coronavirus on our culture, I'm sure, provided some motivation in the organization of stories in this book.

I wrote the first draft of the title story, "The Plague Confessor," in 2018, nearly two years before the virus' advent. But these strange and tragic times often bring me to a meditation of the so-called Black Death — the medieval pandemic in which this story is set.

This story, and the others I have chosen for this book, each in different ways speak to a phenomenon that is born, grows and spreads through a person, a community, a world.

They all convey struggles, and imperfections, perhaps a transformation.

I can only tell you that writing a story can affect a transformation in the writer.

The short stories in this book represent writings over a span of nearly 30 years. I recognize that even acknowledging such a length of time, as a woman, risks a certain liability.

As a writer, and as a grown woman, I feel we grown women ought to be done with apologizing for time's passing, and how much time we've spent so far creating our lives.

Part of my life's creation also lies in stage performance, including dance, and producing events to bring music, dance and literature together.

My work to combine these elements is reflected in the cover art, and the same is true for my recent poetry books.

In all expressions of creativity, I find blessings, and responsibility.

They present ways to share, and to evolve.

One thing that has evolved with time, is technology, and its impact — and for fiction writers, this includes challenges in storytelling.

Stories I wrote in contemporary settings I have opted to keep in those settings.

Stories written and set in the 1990s, for example, reflect the role technology played then, as opposed to now.

For example, I have chosen not to introduce cell phones or text messaging in stories I wrote before their use became prevalent.

I have, however, made slight adjustments and edits, so the context of the period is clear.

And in the timespan of these stories, I've been blessed as a writer by the support of many friends, and family members.

I'm grateful to the editors who chose many of the stories for magazines and other publications.

I'm grateful to Eric Stanway of Emu Books, for our years of professional collaboration, and friendship.

I am always and forever grateful to my husband,

Derek Savoia, for all his support of my dreams; and to my late husband, Lawrence Carradini, poet, scientist and sharer of my journeys for 18 years.

This book is dedicated to his memory, and that of his sister, Eileen, and brother, Ric — three great storytellers, and three great hearts.

— Lowell, Mass., May 11, 2020

Dedication

In memory of
Lawrence Carradini,
his sister **Eileen Herlan,**
and brother **George "Ric" Carradini.**

Voices of beauty guide the starry path.

A Bride Never Waits

Amanda stood in front of her mirror, in her new, smart, lavender suit.

She felt more than a little pride — not only did it look great, it had been on sale.

Just like her tan pumps.

She smiled, and her green eyes flashed.

Her hair was short, straight and cut around her ears, and reddish-blonde.

She gave it a light spritz of hairspray.

It was time.

Amanda had met Richard just a few months before, when summer was in full sway and warm air floated in a dream-like haze.

Mutual friends had invited them to stay-over at a cabin they rented on York Beach. It was a fun time, with volleyball games, and time for walking on the shore.

That, they did, and stayed in touch.

"You could have the whole week, you know," her manager was saying. Amanda forced a smile. She admired many things about Mavis, but her second-guess-ing her employees' decisions was not one of them.

"Well I promise, we will, probably next April."

"That's months away."

"We want to plan for a nice trip," Amanda said.

After a moment, Mavis said: "That's probably wise."

"I appreciated the presents, and the cake. It wasn't necessary."

"It's a special day," Mavis said. "Make it count."

Amanda was anxious to leave. That office was never her favorite place to linger.

The cake. The presents. The fuss. Why had she ever let on to Joyce. Must have been a moment of weakness.

Just two days off. She was used to taking her time off in small increments like that. She had told Joyce, there is always so much, and her work was so specialized, she'd have to train someone, and this she didn't have time to do.

"Everyone's replaceable," Joyce had said, and then — "I mean, everyone deserves time off."

Well, here she was, the beginning of a day free of office chatter and stale cake. Richard, her groom, was waiting.

Amanda knew she was not gorgeous, and she didn't mind. Her precise look agreed with her. Her mother had said, "You have a pleasing look," which she always supposed was a nice way of saying her looks were average.

Amanda did not take offense. She and her mother were close. Her mother lived in a 55-plus apartment complex, Pine Shades. Her mother was welcoming, yet self-reliant.

For her part, Amanda had a small but comfortable, two-bedroom apartment a few blocks away. She could walk to work, and often did.

As she stepped out of the building lobby and onto the sidewalk, a bus wheezed by. A woman pushed a stroller with purpose.

I like living here, she thought. She also relished the organization of her life. She worked hard, had a small but interesting group of friends. Her mother was her best friend. They were after all, two single women, who understood each other.

Over the past few years, since losing her father, they had grown even closer.

Her mother had asked about Richard, and just her asking made Amanda smile. She took out her phone and showed a picture of them — a selfie, but forgiving angles — at the beach party.

"Well," her mother had said. "That's good." They both smiled, almost conspiratorially.

The air of early fall was inviting, even in the city. Amanda saw Richard pulling up to the curb. She liked this about him — his timing was impeccable. He seemed to sense out a parking space just as another vehicle was leaving it. And, he could parallel park with amazing precision.

He got out and approached her, the light of the world in his eyes. He had trim, brown hair, and like her, green eyes.

"We're gonna make pretty babies," he had said one of their dinner dates, after they had agreed to be married. He was exact, yet unhurried. He didn't make demands on her. He didn't make demands, in general. He had a job as an engineer, and his life moved in logical cycles as hers did.

They kissed briskly, and holding hands, began their walk to City Hall.

"I'd go with you," her friend Marcie had said. Marcie was a technical writer, working and living at home, with a wriggly three-year-old, Theresa, on her lap.

"Oh, I couldn't ask that," Amanda said. "You have your hands full. There's a witness there, anyway. The greeter."

"The one with the bracelet charm to ward off the Evil Eye?"

"What?" Amanda blinked. Marcie said such esoteric things. Her fingertips felt cold.

"She got it taking care of a Greek lady," Marcie said. "It's a charm — all over the Mediterranean, they have it."

"Oh," Amanda breathed.

Marcie was a great friend, and her conversations were always enlightening. But, it seemed to Amanda that Marcie's mind was forever wandering through a forest of paths, easily diverted to something interesting but irrelevant.

Thus went their conversation, just a few days before. Amanda had no issue with Marcie, but she simply saw no need for her to be there at the wedding.

Marcie had a beautiful wedding five years earlier, and there were folk singers and a buffet of foods from all over the world. It was at the elegant Country Ledge Inn.

Amanda had enjoyed it. But, today — Amanda's wedding day — was about form, function, endings, and beginnings. A frilly gown and tins of couscous kept warm by a Bunsen burner were not in order.

She and Richard had agreed to a dinner at a nice Italian place; she let Richard pick it, and make the reservations.

—

"What do people at work say?" she asked him as they walked.

"Not much," laughed Richard. "I work in a pod, remember?"

"Yeah, 'course. I have a lot of gossips where I am. I'm glad God invented earphones."

They made some more practical conversation as they walked. Amanda felt herself pulling a bit on his hand.

"Hey, we've got plenty of time!" He laughed again, but sounding slightly uneasy — as if savoring those final moments of bachelorhood, even as they made their way together.

"Mmm, I like to give myself a few extra minutes," she said. She mused to herself, Richard could be forgiven for a fleeting wistfulness as his days as a single man were about to end.

City Hall was in sight. But they had one stop before that, as she had explained to Richard before.

Dolly's Florist, where she would pick up her bouquet. And carry it herself. No pint-sized flower girls with sticky hands from last-minute chocolates.

The front window of Dolly's was a bright array of fall-themed arrangements. The golds and reds were enticing.

A cheery door chime rang as they walked in.

Dolly herself stepped forward to greet them, while her young assistant, Tiffany, was busy on a phone, taking down the details of an order.

"Well, here comes the bride," Dolly said. Her white hair was almost halo-like, and she wore a red dress so festive it looked as if she was on her way herself to a gala event.

"This is Richard," Amanda said, for the first time, beaming.

"Well, aren't you lucky," Dolly said in her sweet, reassuring voice.

"I know it. The beach house. Right place, right time," Richard said. "Synchronicity."

Dolly gave a puzzled glance as if he'd said a word in a foreign language. Amanda shrugged her shoulders and said, "We're ready."

"I can see that," Dolly said, twinkling. "Come on."

"Oh, I can wait out here," Richard said. "I'm already seeing the bride before the wedding, isn't that bad luck?"

"What's done is done," Amanda and Dolly said, almost at the same time. Amanda saw a flash of nervousness cross his face.

Well, of course he's nervous, she thought. A 33-year-old bachelor, about to leave that life forever.

Dolly escorted them through a door behind the cash register. Tiffany kept chatting, leaning over the counter, undisturbed.

"This is like something my mom would do," Richard was saying, as Dolly led them through a narrow corridor at the back of the building. In contrast to the front of the store, it was a tight, and dull space, with wood paneling on the hallway walls from some sad, distant age.

"Mom always like to build suspense, especially before a big day," Richard said.

Neither Dolly nor Amanda answered him.

Dolly opened another door, and the inside was black. "Used to be part of an old theater," Dolly said.

"Ah," Richard offered. His hand, still holding Amanda's, felt warm and sure, but Amanda noticed his breath growing shallow.

A crimson light seemed to fill the space. To their left was a woman, who might have been a ringer for Amanda but she was a bit taller. The man whose arm she clutched was not like Richard. He was short, and great pools of sweat on his forehead gleamed in the light.

There were others. Comically, Amanda thought, this lot almost looks like clumsy middle-schoolers arriving at a dance. Like people who went just because their parents made them.

Each man, or woman, was in the grip of their escort.

They'd been told different stories to lead them here. After all, everyone going to City Hall to get married would have looked very odd to the city clerk.

They'd entered through different places. All going in through a florist shop — well, that would have just looked ridiculous.

The florist shop was one of many portals. A bank, a corner grocery, an insurance office.

Like arteries of the city, leading to its heart — its hungry heart.

Amanda never thought much about it, only the car-

rying out. Her last engagement had simply "broken off."
She received no more than the token pity of a woman in
her 30s still searching for the perfect partner.

Richard shifted and struggled for a bit, but as with
the others, his movement grew stiff and slack. This was
why no one seemed in a hurry to run or try to escape.
In the chill, red mist, they could not. Once they inhaled,
it made quick work of every sensor declaring fight, or
flight.

They were all gathered, in a ragged horse shoe shape,
around a table. They were numb in the haze they inhaled, yet everyone who had brought them there was
fine.

Amanda had a moment of reservation that quickly
subsided. Richard, on the long table, his shirt open to
reveal skin that was pathetically white — not the fresh
bronze of their beach house meeting. That almost made
it necessary.

Dolly in her red dress, with its incongruous holiday
flair, seldom offered explanations, because at this point,
there would be no need. But Dolly wasn't always pre-
dictable. "It takes a lot to keep a city running. It takes a
village to raise a child. It takes a child to give back."

Dolly handed Amanda a stylus that gleamed slightly.

Richard's eyes pooled with useless terror. But even
that was growing dull as his nerves betrayed his eyes,
his brain.

No one screamed. No air moved through those fro-
zen lungs. They could each only stand and watch, until
it was their time.

"You could advance," her mother was saying, as she

and Amanda sat in the bright, cheery kitchen that was a duplicate of all the kitchens in all the apartments in Pine Shades.

"Well, I think it's time to have that talk," Amanda agreed, holding the pink china cup in her hand. "After yesterday, I think I've shown myself."

"Yes, you have," her mother said. "And I'm proud of you."

"Hey, you taught me," Amanda reminded her, patting her mother's arm, still firm. She could feel her mother's quiet strength through the power blue sweater.

"You know, at one time, I even thought you might have been upset at me," her mother said.

"Why?"

"About your father, I mean."

"Oh." After a moment: "I guess by that, I knew. And I knew you were doing it for both of us. So we could remain. And have a place."

"That's why I was so proud of you," her mother said.

Then, "You know, I was reading an article the other day, about the most interesting thing. Advances in testing for DNA. Could solve a lot of crimes."

"Mom," Amanda leaned forward. "It's gonna be okay. First, you have to actually have DNA." Then they both laughed, in the close and inimitable bond of a mother and daughter.

The Plague Confessor

I will begin with the events of The Year of Our Lord, Thirteen Hundred and Forty-Eight, which dawned with prayers for life where we have known only death.

I, Arturo di Taro, am not a man of great standing, but I bring to bear my writing skill, and my training as a solicitor's clerk.

There are men more eloquent, surely.

At least, there were.

But they have taken their eloquence with them to the graves. Stacked, layered, like cheese in a lasagna. I am not the first person to make that comparison.

When the first people took sick, Bishop Sorrino sent priests door to door.

Some refused to go, defying the order.

Even the priests who refused, soon succumbed.

Again and again, the faithful, wiping bloody spittle from their lips, asked the same question:

Why were some allowed to live, and others to die?

I lost my wife, and my daughter. Yet I lived.

It is as if the Angel of Death simply cast about, blindfolded, striking down one and sparing another.

Then, word came from Pope Clement.

It was a notice posted on church doors, and carried by heralds: "If there is no priest, confess to one another. If necessary, confess to a woman."

To ask for an explanation was futile; these heralds moved quickly, their heads covered in hoods that surely became shrouds for some of them.

The absurdity spoke for itself.

After all, this ruling came, as such ecclesiastical pronouncements had for some time, from the papal residence of satin, scarlet, and lavish banquets, in Avignon, France.

In truth, many wondered, if His Holiness brought this disaster upon his people by refusing to return to the rightful seat of the church, in Rome.

Answers, such as there were any, lay with those laid to rest in choked cemeteries and even in river beds. Meanwhile, the pope remained sequestered in his French sanctuary, with only great fires around him for company, as prescribed by his physician.

But, here, in Piazza della Rosa — my home since childhood, a quiet residential district in Florence — walls echoed with coughs, and wails of mourning.

I had a friend, Tomaso di Marcho Spinellini, who I saw, gazing at the edict, wraps of linen pulled around his face, and shaking his head.

He was a good man, a man who lived by the letter of law. If anyone would linger outdoors, to ponder the posting of the pope's emergency ruling, it would be he.

I saw Tomaso di Marcho Spinellini from my window.

I did not go out, though my heart broke for an embrace of one who was so like a brother to me. He turned. I saw the consternation in his eyes — once bright, now filmed like a polluted river.

What woman would go door to door, in times of good health, or bad?

Tomaso di Marcho Spinellini held up a hand to wave. I did, and we both made a vague sign of the cross to one another.

Then, his shoulders rose and fell as his body sighed. He turned, back to the direction of his own home.

I do not know if he made any final act of contrition to anyone, man, woman, child — or perhaps the stray geese now padding about the street, indifferently.

My persistence in my habits and training, of keeping a fastidious diary, with dates and recollections, anchored me to any workable sense of time.

Without my family — my wife's laughter, her singing when she thought none of us could hear her, my daughter, saying, "Ah mama, I promise we won't listen!" all other markers of the life cycle seemed to cease.

I let our cat into the house. She was a fine hunter of rats.

But, the screech and scratch of their mortal dance now seemed ill met. Once I let her in, she ventured out only fervently. It was not long before I began singing to her, as my wife had once sung to some invisible, angelic audience.

No more heralds came.

At night, distantly, there sometimes came the crackle of fire, churlish laughter, and absurdly, the playing of a lute or tamborine, and song. Not my wife's beatific song, but vulgar, tavern verses.

I knew what was happening. Those of us left to take stock of anything, knew what it was.

There were those who simply grew tired of staying inside; they went out, in ragged, stumbling bands, having broken into the wine stores of deceased vintners. As they staggered, laughing, through the streets and down alleys, their numbers grew.

This raucous mob would simply drift into the houses of the deceased, take anything of value, gorge themselves on food stores, and give themselves over to whatever pleasures they might enjoy before death came for them, too.

But I adopted a posture of vigilance.

Even without my family and only a cat for company, I was not about to surrender my goods or my life.

Visitors became a thing of the past, and with such disorder about, the prospect of visitors was not a welcome one.

So it was when one day, I heard a knock at my door.

I peered out the window at first, and then drew back, shaking my head.

I caught myself looking down at the cat, lying in an arch in a rare spot of sunlight, as if she could explain.

I wasn't inclined to answer the door for anyone in those days. But, the knock was followed by a curiously soft voice, like a wisp of vapor in the morning air.

I drew a scarf close to my face, and took my stave in one hand.

I opened the door.

Standing there was a slight girl — young but with the wizened look of a grandmother,, with a thin, gauze scarf about her head.

It took me a moment, but then, the recognition came to me like a flash of sun between clouds.

Her name was Caterina, and she was a prostitute.

"Signor," she said. "Forgive my intrusion. I am looking for the home of a man named Bartolomeo di Nardo."

I thought, but did not ask aloud — Why would Bartolomeo di Nardo be seeking the company of a prostitute so indiscreetly?

The social order was truly eroding, I marveled. That these transactions occurred was a fact of life — that they would happen so brazenly surely signalled a greater breakdown, just like the intoxicated burglars.

But Caterina herself gave the answer.

"His wife is pleading for someone to hear his confession," Caterina said.

I pointed across to his house. She thanked me and turned to go.

Over the course of the next few weeks, I noticed something.

The roads, the streets had gone mostly quiet, except for the wails, day and night, of those who had lost yet another family member.

Men went out with carts, rags tied about their mouths, and those who had the strength carried out their dead. They were taken to the grounds where they were buried one atop the other.

It was not long before this too ceased, and bodies went into the river — another practice now allowed by distant papal edict.

I did not venture out much myself, except when necessary, such as to go the market. I soon stopped doing that, because there was no market.

I ate vegetables from my own garden, and took in a pheasant or duck when I could.

Still, I kept watch, as I am sure many were doing. I kept watch as to who was outside. Houses where no one had survived had been burgled, even ransacked. And who was to say these hoodlums wouldn't soon prevail upon houses of those still living.

I was ready, all the time.

But, after that perfunctory arrival at my door, I now saw Caterina from time to time, alone, making her rounds.

Caterina, going in and out of those houses, hearing the dying in their pleas for forgiveness and absolution. It was as if God had spared her for this purpose.

Not long after Caterina started on her strange new vocation, there was another knock at my door.

This visitor, too, was a woman, the daughter of a well-to-do family for whom I had drafted documents of property and asset transfers some years ago.

She was Signora Veronica di Gentile Altoviti, and she was the lone adult survivor in her family.

Her husband had died; I remember attending his funeral when proper funerals could still be held.

Then, her father succumbed. Her mother had long since died, in childbirth to Veronica.

Veronica, it seemed, was now alone. But, she had inherited all of her family's property and assets.

From the look on her face, I could see that was of little consolation.

In time, to any of us working in the legal profession, it would become clear. There were women surviving, alone, who stood to inherit their husband's and family's estates.

Either the plague was bringing the world to an end, or a curious new world to a beginning.

"Signor," she said. "Forgive the intrusion. I have come to see if anyone here is in need of medical assistance."

"Thanks be to God, I am well," I told her. "He has seen fit to take my wife and daughter, and so they are beyond the need of any medicine."

"I am sorry, Signor," she said. "I remember them well. I saw them often at Mass. I am sure they are with the angels."

Then, she paused. "People are saying it is God's displeasure. That the world is done."

"Has God sent you to look after the dead and dying?" I was genuinely curious, and puzzled.

"The physician can no longer do it," she said. "And his assistants are themselves ill, or simply refuse."

"How can they refuse those who are ill?"

She sighed, and for the first time, tears pooled in her eyes, and grief showed through her resolve. "Signor, I must tell you. You surely know. If you could see what I have already seen. Mothers and fathers are fleeing their own children."

"Merciful God," I breathed.

I am looking for those children, who are left alone. For whatever reason God has seen fit to spare me, so I am doing what I can for them."

"I will send word to your home, if I hear of those in need," I pledged.

"That is all I ask, and thank you," she said, turning to leave.

As she walked away, alone, her pace steady with purpose, I saw Caterina approach her. I watched the two women stop and talk to each other. They were a bit far for me to hear what they said.

I looked out at the two covered, graceful figures disappearing over the hill. It seemed they had decided to travel on together. That made sense. And, clearly, it was safer.

That night, I lay sleepless, and my conscience weighed heavily.

For a woman to be walking without male protection, even in the best of times, was inviting trouble. What if they were to encounter those same toughs who had laid waste to so many empty homes?

They were brave. Braver than I. I looked at the cat, getting up and moving to follow her patch of sun, as if she could somehow assuage my growing sense of guilt.

The next day, I went to Veronica di Gentile Altoviti's home; I remembered it from visiting with my law partner, to examine her father's papers.

No servants answered. They, too, were gone, or too ill. It was Veronica herself who came to the door.

That shocked me, even as I was growing accustomed to things that might no longer prove shocking.

"Signor di Taro," she said. "It's good of you to come. Have you heard of someone in need."

"I have not," I said. "But, if I may come in."

Between us, an awkward, ungainly silence lingered. Then, after furtively looking to each side, her eyes took on an expression almost akin to a smile.

"Of course." She opened the door, and I stepped into what had once been a grand, gay, sunny space. Windows were closed, as mine were, as were most windows everywhere.

Shadows fell across the floor, obscuring the bright red carpets of Turkey and Persia that the family proudly claimed. Candles provided the only light, and the air was fetid.

I realized, it was not unlike my own home, minus expensive carpets.

"Signora, I must approach a subject I pray will not give offense," I said.

"Please sit," she said, her eyebrows knotted, her face a puzzle even in the gloom. We sat in dark, oak chairs. "I apologize, I have no wine to offer."

"Signora, there is no need to apologize," I said. Who was there to press the wine, or casket or sell it? Who was there to break bread, to harvest crops? I wondered if those of us so far untouched by plague would face a slower death by hunger.

I drew a sharp breath. "It concerns me that you are here alone," I said.

Unexpectedly, she laughed. A clear, pure laugh — a sound I thought surely I would never hear again.

"Signor, if you are concerned for my reputation, I hardly think anyone is left to gossip or comment. Everyone knows my husband and father died and it is no fault of mine, or anyone's."

"Do you feel safe here?"

"This is my home. I grew up here. Signor, I am touched, but, I think you will find there are others in greater need."

I left shortly after this. Veronica, young and widowed. Both of us. robbed of our spouses and families by this pestilence.

Out on the road again, I encountered a familiar face, and a welcome one.

Abbot Lorenzo di Soto was the head of a monastery, and one that was rapidly emptying as the monks fell to sickness. The abbot was coarse and stout, and known for speaking his mind.

"Signor di Taro," he said. What a welcome sound. Simply the sound of another human voice, in friendly greeting, was a blessing.

"Good day, Father di Soto," I said. "I have come from the di Gentile Altoviti estate."

"Ah. A sad story, that," he nodded.

"I pray you will find the time to stop there. I fear for the Signora di Gentile Altoviti, alone and without protection."

"That is a story I am hearing many times," he said. "I will of course. But, look at me, signor. I am a fat, old monk too much given to good meat — when it was available. I would not be much of a match for any hoodlums who came upon her house."

"Leave some sign that would give pause for thought," I said. I was about to say, place a crucifix outside the gated entrance, and then thought of the houses and even churches bearing these once-respected signs — many of which were simply torn down, maybe even melted down.

Prayers, displays of relics, penitents lying prostrate on stone steps — none of this, after all, had discouraged the pestilence in its course.

He looked down at his palms, as if seeking an answer there.

"I recall, once, on a pilgrimage to the Holy Land, I met with the Arab physicians there. This kind of sickness was not unknown to them. They said there was a theory that it is transmitted from one person to another, invisibly, through the air," he said.

Before I could ponder this odd turn of discussion, he answered, to himself more than to me.

"It makes more sense than what others are saying. Who does God have to punish here? If God is angry at anything it is the fact that we have a pope who is in France, instead of in Rome, where he should be."

It was always this monk who said what others surely thought.

"I'm hearing complaints about this girl, going around, and hearing confession," he went on.

Caterina. I drew a sharp breath before I could stop myself.

"Signor, in the end, it's no more absurd than invisible particles spreading pestilence in the air. I cannot be everywhere to comfort everyone. If a woman could do it, then so be it," he said. "Such a woman anointed the feet of our savior."

After we parted ways, his last words lingered with me.

Everyone knew the Gospel story — the woman of ill repute, who washed Christ's feet and brought him refreshment, even as learned and holy men watched in bewilderment.

A few days later, the church bells rang, mournfully, rung by a lone steward, and its shambling tolls were for the abbot who loved good food, and spoke the truth.

I wondered if, in his own final moments, if he had barked hoarsely at the steward to call Caterina to his bedside — shattering the last vestiges of some arbitrary moral conduct.

Uttering regrets for her ears only his gluttony, the times his blunt tongue may have bruised, or whatever other faults he might exorcise with his dwindling strength.

Now and then, horse-drawn carriages could be sent, with furniture tied up hastily; some were simply leaving, as if for a new, unspoken land somewhere, with green hills free of plague.

I wondered about those far-away Arab physicians. And our own physicians, who advised eating only lettuce, or making sure to change one's sleeping positions to keep the heat of the body in balance.

Some said a person could invite the disaster upon themselves by dwelling too long in thought on the illness.

The mayor and his councilors were growing frustrated. At last, he declared that the bell-tolling must cease. How was anyone to stop thinking about the plague, if there were endless expressions of grief?

So even the least modicum of dignity and comfort

was now taken from those who needed it most — the dying, and their families.

He ruled that anyone found to be fleeing the city, and leaving a sick family member behind, would be stopped and fined. Strong words, but more than once I saw coins being pressed into the hands of those deputized with this job. And then those abandoning the sick and dying, were free to pass.

Through all this, Signora di Gentile Altoviti, and Caterina, still ventured out, going where they could, and doing what they could.

If there were those leaving here in search of a better life, some were coming here from elsewhere.

Talking of medical remedies had altogether ceased. Those who lived took one of two approaches. They either shut themselves away in quiet, prayerful piety.

Or, they went another way — throwing parties, sometimes in the middle of the street, dancing in circles, holding hands, and drinking wine stolen from abandoned homes.

The di Gentile Altoviti estate was imprinted on my mind — as if by mental will, I could keep these dregs away from the di Gentile Altoviti gate, and from the Signora.

By morning, it was not unusual to see the corpses of the revelers, fallen down, ragged and broken.

Their bodies lay where they fell, until the gruff mountain people charged with picking them up in carts came, and dispatched them to the river.

And then, as before, long spells of silence.

I stayed within my house, as much as I could; my few

remaining friends, after all, were gone.

I wrote, and wrote. I aired my fears to my cat, so all the outside world could go on thinking a brave man lived here. Quiet, stalwart, brave.

I numbered the days as they passed. The slanting light of the sun, and subtle change in the air that made its way indoors, or that greeted me in my walled garden.

It was there, on such a crisp morning, that it occured to me.

I had not seen in some time, the Signora di Gentile Altoviti — or Caterina.

I looked back upon my records, looking for the last dated entry that mentioned either one of them.

It was not long, however, before the Signora di Gentile Altoviti came to my door once more. She was in tears.

I ushered her inside — as she had once observed, there was no one left to pass judgement on such an impropriety.

"What is wrong?"

"Signor di Taro, it seems you haven't heard. The mayor has issued another edict."

"Why, what now?" It seemed a cruelty of God's design that so many good people were gone, and the mayor, seemingly bankrupt of any kindness, remained with us.

"There are a few surviving magistrates who have said that it is the city's own loss of morals," she said. "They are forcing the beggars and prostitutes out of the city."

Caterina.

Before I could say anything, she said, "I was there, when it happened. Some men came, and they forced

Caterina into a carriage with some other women. I tried to stop them, but they just...pushed us aside."

I felt a rage rise within me. "Where did they take them?"

"I do not know. I think they will throw them out of the city, and anyone caught letting them back in will likewise be removed," she said. "Signor, with your legal background, I am hoping you can appeal to the mayor about this."

"I am a cleric. I am not licensed to practice law," I protested, and instantly regretted it.

"Signor," she said, anger filling her voice, "I think we can all attest to the fact that most if not all those licensed to practice law are gone, dead and gone. They cannot profess on behalf of the living, or the dead."

She looked away, as if shocked by her own outspoken manner.

A heavy silence fell between us. Then, she turned back, and raised her eyes, meeting mine with a hard resolve.

"Please do not be offended. But, you came offering me protection, and I know from your dealings with my father that you are an honest and principled man."

Then, she added, slowly. "Caterina said as much to me."

Before I could answer in my surprise, she said, "I would have asked the abbot. But, as you know, he is gone, as well."

Lamely, I said all I could think to say: "Signora, I will have a look at my law books, and see what I can do."

"That's all I ask," she said, but tears formed brightly in

those unwavering eyes.

That was the end of the matter, and we both knew it.

Gone. Police, lawyers, clergy, craftsmen, farmers. Survivors, such as ourselves, trying to weave feeble strands of order back together.

The mayor, calling on magistrates from other cities, in an effort to keep some semblance of governance.

And looking for someone to blame.

In my daily log, I had one furtive entry of seeing Caterina face to face, a few weeks after she came to my door.

It seemed we both had our eyes on the same plump, errant goose.

Without my asking, she told me she had chosen her profession because her husband had left her, with two children. And, then, the plague claimed them for its own.

She turned confessor, because she, and the sick, were outcasts, all.

And, she had said, in her pain fashion, what was there for a prostitute to do. There was no more clientele, and those alive, were simply trying to keep alive.

But, the families of the abandoned, seeking final absolution, were passed judging, she said. They gave her from what bread or milk they had. They all prayed and cried together.

But even these ones, I realized, would be in no position to argue for her case, even if they were inclined.

If they were even strong enough to make the journey to the city offices, to stand at a docket, they would be immediately turned away and perhaps even fined for risking the spread of more sickness and death.

And an attorney would be of no help in any case — because people were living by their own laws now.

It would matter little that this same woman had prepared so many souls to stand at the threshold of Heaven.

She was what she was, and so had been carted off with so many of her sisters in trade.

As the weather changed, it brought other changes. More and more, I began to hear voices in the street — strands of greeting or discussion, here and there.

Those who lived began to venture out more, however tentatively.

And, the plague, wherever it went, sent those evicted by landlords, or those who simply thought life must be better elsewhere, onto roads, into new and unfamiliar places.

These travelers brought news. Some of it was sadly familiar — tales of death, and disorder.

But some news was startling, and strange.

Roaming bands of young men and women were taking up a new cause. Imitating the sufferings of Christ, they walked, prayed, sang and flogged themselves.

They began to attract followers. They even ambushed local parishioners, sometimes throwing out the priests and taking over, promising a deliverance that the churchmen had not.

There came news that caused a great chill surpassing the horrors we survivors had already witnessed.

When the sickness persisted even after the prostitutes and beggars were ushered out, some cast about for others to blame.

They set upon Jewish merchants and businessmen — including some I knew, from business dealings — often tearing them off a horse or carriage, and dragging them before courts.

One story I heard often was an accusation of poisoning well water.

Some people accepted this explanation. Even as the Florentine cardinal observed that everyone, Jews, and Christians alike, drank from the same wells.

It mattered not. In cities across Italy, Germany and France, the Jews were being strapped to stakes, and set alight, leaving behind land and goods readily confiscated.

And, debtors who no longer owed notes to Jewish creditors.

Those who related this tale bore a grim disgust in their eyes. The same people who thought God had unleashed punishment for material decadence now seemed poised to reward them with the assets of those who died on these pyres.

Perhaps the end of the world had surely come, after all.

But, it hadn't.

The dying stopped, flaring sporadically, but not a terrible, dark wave, as before.

Even more amazingly, young women and men began to think of a future, and began creating it. They married, and started to have children.

The mayor gave up his office, abruptly announcing a longing to retire as a private citizen.

It was resignation that prompted cynical smirking —

it was all well since an indictment evaporated with his departure.

After all, none of his purges of so-called undesirables, or his orders to silence the bells, had cured the sick, or risen the dead.

I wondered, too, if the time had come for a new beginning.

The Signora di Gentile Altoviti had only one surviving male relative that I knew of, an uncle. I went to him, to request her hand in marriage.

A few days later, he came to my home, and said he was sorry but the Signora di Gentile Altoviti was not of a mind to marry again, at least not now.

Indeed, she was only one of a number of widows, or bereft women, some with one or more estates or dowries.

I found work in mediating disputes between many of these dowagers and their workmen, who now were demanding higher wages and better housing for their families.

There were new beginnings, and not all were to everyone's liking.

I'm not a master gamesman, never have been, but on occasion, I have enjoyed such an outing; the public forest glens could prove soothing, and an escape from the cares of life in the city.

I went on such an outing, more for the clarifying of my mind and soul, than in search of pheasant or grouse.

I left the path of my fellow marksmen for a time. A forest of ferns laced the slender beams of sun through their delicate fronds.

I stopped. My eyes blurred, and I could not comprehend what I was seeing, on the ground, trailed by leaves, and a halo of flies.

There was the loose soil falling over bone. Everyone had become accustomed to such sights, with so many unfortunates not properly buried.

But this was not one of those. The strands of the hood were still wrapped partly around the head, the crown of the skull.

Caterina. Whether claimed by hunger, or set upon by attackers, I could not say.

My mind flashed back to my conversation with the Signora di Gentile Altoviti. I had said I would try to help Caterina, and I did not.

The other men in the party were calling for me, distantly.

I knelt in the muddy earth.

"Bless me," I said through clasped, tear-drenched hands.. "For I have sinned."

A Boy with Pretty Eyes

*For "Turbo Tom" McKittrick and
His Freak Show Extravaganza*

"There's a lot of play with the muscles that hold the eyeball," Ben said, in that knowing tone of voice that had long ago alienated him from most of his fifth-grade class.

Here, during the class science demonstration projects, he wasn't about to win them back.

He had decided on this course of action, initially, because it seemed less likely to get him beat up than did showing his homeroom how an abacus works.

He reached into the front pocket of his jeans, which sagged on him.

He pulled out a butter knife.

Before the teacher could stop him, he wedged the knife's spreader-end between his lower eyelid and one of the dark brown eyes — which his grandmother had said would always be his only redeeming features.

One of those two redeeming features was now a free-floating globe, balanced on the edge of the knife's blunt edge.

It was only then that the teacher, Mrs. Bursten, broke from her stupefying horror, and leapt up from her desk to escort Ben to the nurse's office.

Inches off her chair, however, she froze once again, as if Ben's disconced miracle of sight had shot a paralyzing beam through her.

She thumped back onto her chair, and gazed at him, her face shiny, her mouth open but petrified, and something between shock and ardor in her eyes.

Vaguely, she heard gasps, cries, perhaps the thud of someone fainting, and then, applause from the rows of spellbound students.

Ben rather unceremoniously popped his eyeball back into his socket, as if pocketing a marble, and made a campy bow before returning to his seat.

The display was disgusting, but effective. Ben had won the day.

Later, no one minded at all when Ben sat with them at lunch; in fact, he got a few nervous invitations, some of them from girls.

At least at lunch, talking could be limited by eating. When he did talk, however, he flitted away from the subject of his show-and-tell trick. He knew somehow, that revealing its details would give away its power, a power for the first time ever in his grasp.

This somewhat befuddled his classmates, who expected some long, gurgling, pedantic, and frankly, Ben-like explanation.

And fundamentally, Ben really didn't know fully why or how he could do the trick.

He knew that eye-popping was an old circus trick, and that nowadays, some freak artists could still do it.

Ben suspected his ability had something to do with

the other things he'd been able to do lately.

It had all started in the shower.

As he raised one arm, using his free hand to probe for any possibility of hairs growing, his abdomen yawned — and what he was pretty sure were his intestines tumbled out in a graceless, ropy pile.

The shower water spattered over them. They smelled.

For sheer lack of knowing what else to do, Ben leaned over, gathered them up and forced them gracelessly back into the space where they had been coiled up as they should be.

Ben stood, shaking in the pummeling, hot water. When his tremor subsided, and movement churned in his limbs again, he lifted a trembling hand to his chest.

His heart hammered, as if in protest, but in the next moment, it capitulated.

The water drops licked at the pulsing, sighing red blossom. He felt like nothing so much as the prayer-card pictures of Mary and Jesus tucked into the frame of his grandmother's china hutch — their smiling beautiful faces belying their exposed, wounded hearts.

Far from being repulsed, Ben found himself fascinated. Imagine — getting to see, and hold, his own heart, admire its workings, its intricacy, its glory. How it labored, every day, invisibly, at its one task — of keeping him alive.

He stared at it, lovingly, until the water from the shower head began to grow tepid, and his younger sister began to slam her fists into the door — insisting she had to get in because she'd tried to wash their cat with pudding.

He pressed his heart back into place, in its niche within his ribs.

He cranked the handle to turn off the water and stood, just for a moment, feeling a great, rare pride.

He had vaguely thought of following up the eye-removal with the display of his heart, but thought better of it — the eye trick might impress them all, gross them out a bit, but the heart — that might just give a bully or two an idea.

And there was only one other kid in the class on which they would vent their bullyish urges, and for all he knew, that might even try it on that kid.

Worse, that kid was a girl.

Brenda Toomey.

Brenda didn't look especially nerdy, whereas Ben, with his large, girlish brown eyes and black hair perched on his head like a sleeping sea urchin — always did.

Nothing about Brenda, on first inspection, cast her as in any way awkward, or out of step with the ordinariness of the rest of their class. Her clothes were reasonably fashionable, in a fifth-grade girl sort of way.

She wore glasses, but at that point in time, glasses had become sort of "in," even for, and maybe especially, for girls.

What collapsed her fragile facade of conformability was that, when anyone tried to talk to Brenda — and that was not often — she never seemed to be listening.

And when she was, she only wanted to talk about one thing — bugs.

And her penchant for correcting could outpace his, at least when it came to bugs.

"Bugs, Ben." He'd tried to approach her one day, at the beginning of the school year. He tried to impress her by showing her a beetle and declaring, "Look, Brenda, it's one of your bugs."

"Bugs, Ben." It was like some weird mantra. "Ben, you have to understand. If you're going to talk to me about bugs, you should know — that's not a bug."

He had stood helplessly, pointing at the sturdy brown beetle, casting a ridiculously tall shadow on the parking lot in the morning sun.

"Bugs are a family of insects," she continued, her glasses shifting slightly on her nose bridge as she talked.

The beetle trundled on.

Ben looked down on it.

"Ben!"

He looked up sharply. Only his grandmother commanded him with such a voice.

"Ben! It's like this. All bugs are insects. But not all insects are bugs."

No, "thanks for showing me that beetle," no nothing. Just a lecture on bugs and insects, which he didn't quite understand. He'd watched her walk — nay, flounce — into the doorway, as if mixing in blithely with the other girls, which, of course, she couldn't.

His face flushed with rage. Rage at her ingratitude, rage at her nerve to lecture him, as if seizing from him his crown of knowing things others didn't and couldn't know.

Up to now, in the school year, he had resolutely refused to talk to her — about bugs, or insects, or eyeballs, or anything.

Let her sit alone; it was harder to be a girl nerd than a boy nerd, he knew, sensed. Boys were expected to do weird and horrifying things, sometimes. Girls never were.

But liking insects didn't mean she didn't have feelings — about the future, about the world, maybe even about someone she might like someday.

When she wasn't safe within the sanctuary of her daydreams — of becoming a leading entomologist — she had heard invariable snickers — that she and Ben would make a great couple.

The idea irritated them both, but Brenda, less so.

However, that snickering all ceased with the day of Ben's eyeball trick.

Brenda was one of the few girls who didn't exhale in horror at the display.

And since then, the teacher, Mrs. Bursten, had come to realize just what a jewel she had uncovered in what was hitherto the most profoundly irritating child in her entire teaching career.

She now had a phenomenon.

And she began to capitalize on that phenomenon, parading him through the science classes of the other grades in the school, and even to the junior high and high school, bridged together in one brick complex.

When the schoolwide talent fair came around, it was Ben's startling eyeball display that won over Shellie Kimball's gymnastic act.

In the girls' room, Brenda heard Shellie crying.

Shellie was not always the nicest girl, to Brenda, or to anyone.

But now Brenda felt a wave of sympathy for her.

The truth was, since the day of the beetle, Brenda had felt a little bad. Ben had tried to reach out, in his own way.

His eyeball trick hadn't grossed her out; she had stared at it with steady coldness.

But it wasn't from disgust or dislike.

Listening to Shellie blubber as she changed out of her gymnast's tights, Brenda felt a grudging acknowledgement of her true feelings for Ben.

Those dark eyes. Those dark eyes that could do a frightening performance.

Maybe that was twice as special.

But, she kept these feelings to herself, or so she thought, nursing them quietly. Surely, she could never tell Ben, as he walked through the hallways, sitting where he would in the cafeteria and even at assemblies.

And because she couldn't tell him, she began to ache with a profound, sad ache.

She thought, no one must know, and no one could know. If she said nothing, then no one would know.

But, she was wrong.

Her brother, Wes, was 16.

Big brother Wes Toomey wasn't sure why his sister's infatuation irritated him.

When he picked up his little sister from school — the only time he could convince his mother to let him take out the car was for such menial errands — he saw her, staring, for several seconds, at that goofy, bristle-headed kid.

Ben. Ben Makem. That was his name.

He'd seen him pull out his own eyeball. It was cool enough, but as far as Wes could tell, it was about the only thing cool about this little ass-bonnet.

But there was Brenda, his younger sister, so much younger than him that she seemed almost like an embryo that got loose before its time. She was staring at this Ben, unaware that her mother had just bought her a beginner's bra — a fact Wes knew because he'd glimpsed it in a bag on a kitchen chair.

All that night, Wes was agitated.

Sleep eluded him.

From beneath his mattress, he pulled out a magazine.

In the magazine, the women in the photos had breasts that defied gravity, in the way that real-life breasts almost never did.

The fact that Wes had such magazines in his possession was no secret.

The tacit agreement with their Dad was that he keep them stowed away, out of reach.

After all, Dad had a stash of his own.

The next morning, his little sister came downstairs, with a look of considerable distress.

Puzzled, Wes looked up from his second bowl of Cap'n Crunch — in his own house, who was to tell him not to eat the same cereal he'd enjoyed since age eight?

Wes saw it, then — the ghostly outline through her shirt. The beginner's bra.

"You'd better hurry," their mother said, her back to both of them as she rummaged through the cabinet over the sink for something.

Brenda climbed into a chair and gestured wordlessly

to her brother for the cereal box.

He handed it to her, then realized he was staring, and not wanting his sister to realize that.

He wasn't a perv, not like that.

No way.

It took her a good 20 minutes to get through that bowl, and he understood what she was doing — stalling.

Probably she didn't want to get on a bus with the other girls — and he couldn't blame her. Some of them were his friends' kid sisters. A pack of little bitchlings.

"Hey, Bren," he said mushily through the cereal. "I could drive you."

His first class didn't start until 9 a.m. She had to be there for 7:30 a.m.

"You may as well," their mother said. A second later, the schoolbus roared past.

She'd missed it.

"Allright." Brenda's voice reflected more reproach than thankfulness.

The whole ride, she was silent, looking through her Little Golden Book of Insects.

Thanks to his little sister, Wes knew the difference between a lady bug and a Vidalia beetle, a grasshopper and a praying mantis, and the weight of the largest bug — "a true bug" — in the universe. (It was a quarter pound.)

And, he wished that he didn't know such things.

He couldn't believe that he had brain calls storing this kind of information.

Bad enough he could remember the names of all three Pointer Sisters, and the words to most of their songs because mom insisted that the car radio stay at her favorite station.

Mom's car — an aging Buick — chugged as he pulled up the school's driveway. "Do you want me to pick you up after school?"

"I guess," she said, very quietly, clutching her book — because she loved it so much, or because she was trying to hide any hint of her beginner bra upon getting out.

She exited without so much as a "thank you." Wes didn't expect one.

He saw the Eye Kid. He saw his sister see the Eye Kid.

He lingered a moment, the car chugging and complaining, before he drove away.

He came for her at 3:30 p.m. Already the sun hung heavy and orange, over the horizon of trees behind the school.

Most of the kids were already gone. Clusters of them were walking home.

Wes pulled up along the sidewalk, in the fire lane with NO PARKING stencilled into the asphalt surface, and looked about for his sister.

Two girls smirked about something as they strolled out of the main school doors together.

They glanced at him and caught him giving them a sneering look. Baby bitches still in bitchy baby training wheels. They'd be a real treat once they hit high school.

They flashed back a look of half-curiosity, half-disdain, before moving to the school's side lawn, and challenging each other to do cartwheels. As if to convey telepathically, Get chucked, you old man teen pervert.

His sister had never done a cartwheel — not that he had ever seen — and she never would. Cartwheels, he knew from enough trips to pick her up, signaled dominance in the preteen girl world.

As did scoring a goal in field hockey, which she would never achieve, either.

Both, like the unwanted insect knowledge, comprised unwelcome fun facts from her preteen life.

He sat with the engine idling, thumbing through the Want Advertiser and circling listings for used Chevrolets. Peripherally, he eyed the car's digital clock, which now said almost 4 p.m.

He breathed out with irritation. Maybe she'd been kept back.

He turned off the ignition with a hard twist and got out of the car, slamming the huge, side door.

He walked up to the main door, but the secretary, Mrs. Bridle — who'd been chief absentee-noticer and all around gatekeeper since his time there — was walking out.

Her eyebrows arched, and she commented on how grown-up he looked since she last saw him.

With just as little tact, she asked him if he still had a crush on Beth Wisnewski (who'd given birth to triplets a few months before, nothing of his doing.) When he asked, she told him smartly, no, his sister wasn't kept behind and didn't have detention — why should she, she was never in any trouble.

With a discerning glare, she conveyed in steely silence — it was the cartwheel turners on the front lawn who were headed straight for the state juvenile facility in a few years' time.

He thanked her brusquely. As he walked away, she

yelled, "Try 'round the back! Sometimes girls go there to practice jump rope!"

Wes very much doubted his sister would be doing that, but he decided to look, anyway.

Maybe the other girls had seen her bra and regarded it as some kind of status symbol, a mystery only girls could fathom.

He supposed that, for all his unsolicited knowledge of cartwheelers and field hockey and quarter-pound bugs, he didn't really understand much about women, of any age.

Making his way to the back, he moved around the perimeter of the building, which had once seemed like a red-brick fortress, an L-shaped armory that a wrecking ball would barely dent.

Now, so many years later, he thought that if he jumped hard enough, he could reach up and graze the roof with his hand.

"I wanna show you because you're the only one who doesn't ask me dumb questions about it."

Wes stopped. His feet quivered, and ice seemed to rush through his veins.

As for Brenda — she could scarcely believe what she was hearing.

In truth, she was growing indifferent to Ben's neat trick, because she'd seen it now about a zillion times.

But she understood that he didn't like talking about it, and now, he'd singled her out to reveal the secret of his strange power.

Brenda's breath quickened, and the palms of her hands misted slightly.

She put down her book bag — which had a giant grasshopper on it — and red lettering that said, "Faneuil Hall, Boston, Mass."

Something had changed in their relationship, and the facade of chilly indifference they both held up, especially around each other, had slowly begun to thaw away.

Ben, once infuriated by being corrected about the difference between the word "bug" and "insect," showed respect because she always could tell a locust from a grasshopper.

But he had bluntly told her, they must keep their new-found affinity a secret from the rest of the school.

Brenda thought this was kind of foolish, but didn't ponder it too deeply. A secret was kind of fun.

And so, they formed a quiet pact. No hanging out together at recess. No sitting together at lunch. Keep a respectful distance, at all times.

So, she had agreed. The other girls — who had glared at her when they saw the outline of her new attire — would surely shred her if they knew she had won the affection of the Eye Kid.

"When we're in junior high next year, it will be different," she'd told him.

Junior high was next year.

But they were still toiling in the present, in fifth grade.

Wes stood, watching, on the grass spread at the back of the school — grass that was startlingly green and thick, as opposed to the dried straggle at the front.

There was his sister, her shadow drawn up impossibly slim and tall in the afternoon sun, fiery light framing her silhouette, with its slight curves.

There was another shadow, lean, like the Bunker Hill monument.

The Eye Kid.

Only, as it turned out, the Eye Kid was also the Heart Kid, the Liver Kid, the Stomach Kid, and lastly, the Brain Kid.

As Wes watched this display, his throat raw and dry, and his own brain signalling spasms of shock, his sister took it all in with a kind of deadpan, nearly clinical interest.

The Eye Kid — the You Name The Organ Kid — wasn't harming his sister in any way. His put-upon brain tried to convey this reality, but the reality of the spectacle in front of him was holding ground.

And in any case, it didn't matter that what he did, he did to himself, and not to her.

The little goof was standing there, behind the school, with his little sister, who was wearing her first bra, taking tiny steps toward womanhood. And there she stood, in her beginner bra, and this — creature — was showing her all his — things. His internal things!

Like, a flasher! He was exposing himself to Wes' kid sister, so innocent and vulnerable in her My First Bra.

It was like a brittle branch snapping inside him. Wes lunged toward the Eye Kid shadow, a shadow all loopy with an extravagant display of lumps, bumps, and cording from the inside out.

Brenda screamed. "Wes — Noooo!"

She leapt, clawing at her big brother's back.

Ben toppled backward, his vacant skull cracking against the brick work of the school wall.

Brenda screamed again. Wes managed to shake her off him, twisting and grabbing her flailing arms, and setting her ungracefully on the emerald, lush grass.

Rolling away from the brick wall and falling over to the ground, Ben looked like some freakish, ancient deity, arms out, internal organs splayed about, like alien tentacles.

His loose spine kicked and bucked like a rodeo bronco, while his brain sat, with sad indifference, in his dirty, smeared hand.

After what seemed an eternity, Brenda fumbled to her knees. Wes saw her tear-stained face register some revulsion as she plucked the delicate gray mass from Ben's hand, wincing as she placed it as delicately as possible back in his opened crown.

Wes felt as if the whole world was swimming around him.

Still on her knees, and sobbing heavily, his sister picked the bits of gravel and pebbles now clinging to the various organs still on display. Then, she began poking and pushing them back into place.

Ben, his face turned upward, his dark brown eyes shining with an unearthly light, gurgled sharp, spittle-thickened breaths.

Brenda now reeked of something like death, her arms, her face, her clothes covered in dark streaks of protoplasmic gook.

Thanks to her efforts, nothing was out of place anymore — everything was tucked in once again, away from the hazardous, outer world.

Ben lay, spasming, but the spasms began to recede,

until he was nearly still.

Wes reached for his sister's shoulders, still shaking with sobs — and then realized he was huddled on the grass beside her.

The darkness was settling; the waning sunlight vanished and the sky loomed, dark and purple.

The swampy stench of human anatomy faded as a chilly wind grew.

Wes' sense of grudging, big-brother authority began to reassert itself, clamoring from the shock that still gripped him.

"We ought to call him an ambulance," he said, which earned him another hateful stare from his sister.

He overlooked it, with his reticent sense of responsibility empowering him to overlook the slight. "Brenda, he needs help. They might be able to save him!"

Again, the poisonous stare — flashing eyes that clearly said, "Murderer."

The wind toyed with her hair, and in the darkness, she looked oddly, ethereally pretty.

Uselessly, Wes implored. "I'm sorry. I really am. I saw him and I thought —"

She moaned a little. No, she did not. A dog, distantly — no, it was Ben.

The Eye Kid.

Ben's fingertips curled slightly, as if his newly reinstated brain was testing some kind of limit — not yet sure it still had complete control over them.

He managed to form a fist — first with the right hand, and then with the left.

The fingers curled fully, and then relaxed, at first,

slowly, and then with more certainty.

His eyelids fluttered.

His ears wiggled. In his whole life, he had never known he could do that.

Breath churned through his narrow, little rib cage.

Wes looked away from him, to his little sister.

She looked fixedly at this slow resurrection.

"I don't like peanut butter," Ben announced, gazing past them both, to the darky sky and the sliver of a moon.

Walking was hard — as if he had metal bars strapped to his legs.

But Ben resisted the big boy's offer to carry him to his car.

He'd just snapped back from what seemed like near death. He wasn't about to ruin the effect in front of Brenda by folding into her brother's arms.

And after all that had just transpired, he didn't trust the guy, anyway.

Ben sat in the back seat of the car; Brenda sat in front, and they were both silent.

When they arrived at Ben's house, however, Wes got out, scrambling around to the side to open the door for him.

Ben did not look up at him as he stepped out.

For the first time since they had all left the school, Brenda spoke, letting herself out of the car, and coming around to him.

"There's a decimals test in two days," she reminded him. "Maybe we could study tomorrow?"

"Uh, sure," Ben said. "Thanks for the ride," he added,

to Brenda, not to Wes. "See yah."

The next day, after school, was to be a taping of the local access cable show, "Talent Time."

Ben awoke that morning, amazingly refreshed, without a trace of pain from yesterday's harrowing events.

Still, walking and moving his arms was a little awkward, as was turning his head from side to side.

But it didn't bother him too much. He sensed that the clumsiness would soon disappear.

The cable TV studio was warm, and bright with lighting.

George Campion, the host of "Talent Time," was possessed of great technical expertise, but was not good at making his guests feel at ease.

Still, his show had a large following, because his producers were good at getting interesting acts.

As the disco music that signaled the show's opening faded, George looked into the camera, gave a cheerful greeting, and then leaned over to Ben. "Ben, I understand you have a most unusual ability."

Ben looked up from the faded patches on his jeans (the jeans he'd insisted on wearing, rather than the suit he'd worn to his cousin's Confirmation) and stared briefly into the gaggle of oily-looking camera eyes.

He looked at Mr. Campion, remembering now that Mr. Campion worked at Rich's Auto. Ben had gone with his mother, and this guy had given her a hard time in a way Ben was sure he wouldn't if it had been his father instead.

This memory prompted anger, and also gave him an opening. "You were rude to my Mom," Ben said loudly.

"So forget it."

He hoped out of the folding studio chair, whose height had annoyed him, and walked off the set.

On the car ride home, he tried explaining to his parents that he couldn't do the eye trick anymore.

He didn't know why. But it would probably mean glasses later on if he kept doing it, right?

His father drove them in angry silence. There had been a cash prize in play — enough to cover the deductible for the braces Ben was going to need soon.

His mother was silent, too, but her breathing was relaxed. Ben could tell she wasn't angry in the least. Far from it.

The next day at school, almost everyone knew that Ben the Eye Kid had called it quits.

Whether he had chickened out at the TV taping, or just simply didn't want to do it anymore, didn't seem to matter.

Brenda was waiting for him in the home room. "We were going to study today," she reminded him. "Decimals."

He stammered for a moment, and said, "Yeah."

Her look was queerly coy, and slightly petulant.

At lunch, she didn't say anything about the TV fiasco, and Ben didn't bring it up, but he sensed that he didn't have to.

She didn't say a word about his ability, at all. She didn't say a word about everything that had happened that afternoon behind the school.

They were sitting together. She insisted upon it. He found himself concurring.

No one said anything to either of them. They walked past them, trays in hand, without a teasing look or snide remark.

They ate, in agreeable silence, until she asked him if he wanted to come over and see her ant colony.

"Then we could study," she added quickly.

"What about your brother?" Now he thought he heard some unpleasant chorus in the background, about the two of them.

Brenda put down her napkin, almost like a gauntlet. "He's okay."

The much-awaited start of junior high came. With it, came the first dance of the new school year.

A get-acquainted dance — Wes remembered this tradition well.

Harvey Fitz and he had stormed out to the teacher-chaperones' cars, to Mr. Underhill's weird, brown Volkswagen. Spray cans in hand, they'd christened the car, "whale shit."

Each took a word; Fitz misspelled whale as "wail," ruining the effect entirely.

Now it was his sister's time. She and her beau were up to no such trickery.

She had grown an inch taller, and had gotten in the habit of wearing dresses.

The kid formerly known as the Eye Kid had also grown a bit taller, but Wes knew he could still enjoy about one more year before his voice started cracking mercilessly.

The two of them sat in the back seat of Wes' new-used Chevy. While he chauffeured them, he reminded them of the pick-up time. 9:30 p.m. sharp.

He could see the tops of their heads in the rearview mirror. He was sure they weren't doing anything, maybe gently holding hands, and almost surely flipping through Brenda's new field guide to spiders.

His sister's interest in insects had ebbed slightly, and she was making the transition to the things that ate them.

As he pulled up to the door of the school gymnasium, he reminded them again about the pickup time.

His sister said, "Okay, Wes."

After she got out of the car, she looked in the driver side window, and smiled with grace.

She seemed accustomed to his gestures of protectiveness.

He watched them walk serenely toward the gymnasium, holding hands, and carrying themselves in a way that seemed sure of thwarting bullies and the bitch crop alike.

It was a mild September night. Wes drove away with the window down. The evening breeze fluttered the page of the spider guide, which Brenda had left, lying face-up in the back seat.

When a Cat Went Missing

Wet leaves were plastered to the brick sidewalk. It had rained for three days.

At a bus shelter, amidst an archipelago of graffiti, was a poster: LOST CAT.

The cat, named Sammy, was a plumpish tabby.

In a photo, Sammy was plopped on a cushion, his eyes closed, not appearing at all like the errant, adventure-going type.

The poster, rippled from the humidity, said Sammy was microchipped, had been missing since the beginning of May. The poster included a phone number.

It was one of several posters of Sammy appearing around town, in store windows, in a coffee shop, on the bulletin board of the library.

Many who saw the poster would snap a photo on their cell phones, and distribute to their friends on social media or in email groups.

This was not the first time many of them had done this for a lost cat or dog poster.

Sammy looked truly majestic and serene in his picture setting. The thought of such a content, easy-going cat out in a downpour such as this, away from a loving family, caused pain in more than one heart.

In a modest duplex home, Sammy's owners, Carl and Beth, were rising, going to their respective jobs, and returning at night, greeting each other with spare words, the silence of their grief between them.

Sammy had been gone for two weeks now.

Sammy's very being in their household was a significant milestone.

He arrived about two years earlier, then not much more than a kitten. He was one of a fluffy group of orphaned kittens, found abandoned in a box near the Collingsville commuter train station, and taken to a Caring Paws, a shelter.

Sammy and his littermates were bottle-fed by volunteers, and their availability for adoption announced in the local newspaper.

Carl and Beth had retreated from one another after a quarrel, and not the only one in those fragile first months of their relationship.

It was hard now for either of them to remember much about the fight, except that Carl's ex-girlfriend, Cindy, kept interjecting comments in their social media exchanges, usually when it concerned a restaurant.

Beth insisted Carl rid himself of Cindy — as a social media contact, as a presence in his life.

Cindy and Carl hadn't seen each other in person since high school.

She was a remnant of the past, Beth argued. It mattered not that Cindy had been there when Carl's mother had died of esophagial cancer.

That had been kind of Cindy, but that was in a different lifetime.

Let — her — go, Beth said.

With a sharp sigh, Carl did.

Then, at an office cookout, Carl's coworker Ben mentioned that Cindy had emailed Carl at work.

Beth told Carl to leave. He did for three nights, staying at his father's house — two men now without partners, in a dark, chilly ranch house across town.

Carl did not know how to make amends.

He could have asked his father, but his father was caught up in his own struggles, with solitude, with diabetes.

Cindy had remained a friend to his family. His ties to her were mostly of gratitude.

They went to the junior semi-formal, and that was when things ended between them.

Now, they were both in their mid 20s, both with adequately-paying but marginally satisfying jobs.

Their paths had diverged.

Carl's life revolved around his work at Motor Dynamics, and around Beth, who worked in customer service in a department store.

He didn't fully understand Beth's discomfort about Cindy.

But he did remember his father's one bit of advice about keeping a harmonious household: Choose your battles, otherwise you will lose the war.

Carl wanted to repair whatever harm he'd done. And, he wanted to win the war.

He knew Beth liked cats. He liked them, or could at

least tolerate them. Seeing the Caring Paws' post on social media, announcing Sammy the cat's quest for a new home, Carl went to the shelter, applied for adoption, and was accepted.

He went home with Sammy, now fully weaned and ready for solid food, in a cardboard, portable cat carrier, with a blanket and some toys.

To Beth, Sammy signified a milestone that made her heart overflow. Sammy symbolized permanence, of a commitment to the present. He brought the two dissonant parties together.

They could officially call themselves a family.

Two years passed, uneventfully but with stability and logic. Sammy grew affectionate, and, given more to naps than running around, he grew generous in girth.

Then, one night, Carl left his phone on the coffee table; it lit up, and Beth picked it up to answer it.

It was Cindy. Her name flashed on the phone screen. Beth grabbed it, answered it, and heard a shocked breath followed by silence.

Beth sat on the couch, feeling light-headed. She remembered how a coworker had grimaced, then forced a smile, when she said Carl had come back to her and got her a cat.

She felt flushed, absurd, and amazed at her own short-sightedness, at her heart given over so quickly because of a cat.

Carl came into the living room, eating from a bag of pretzels. He then saw her face.

He turned, and went to the door. That's when the rage exploded inside Beth.

Carl opened the door, and before either of them could stop him, Sammy, who never showed the slightest interest in the world beyond his warm abode, departed in a pudgy, gray blur.

The next day, Carl created the 'lost cat' poster at work, and put it on social media. Without alluding to the phone call fiasco, the post simply said he and Beth were heart-broken and wanted Sammy back.

Carl also posted the notice to a 'lost cat' group, and 'help find my pet,' among others.

It was only then he realized the scope of the problem. So many posts about missing pets, especially cats. Dogs could be leashed of course; cats seldom were.

So many posts said, "he/or she is an indoor-only cat, not used to the outdoors."

Two weeks passed.

From time to time, someone would send one of them a photo, in a text message, asking, "Is this him?"

It never was.

Sammy knew all about missing. He knew all about missing time.

He knew all about grief, life and death, because he'd been through it all before.

He carried within him generations of names, and generations with no name.

He carried within him, dingy alleys, sunny meadows, a cold, bitter December with the clatter of horse hooves rushing by.

He carried time.

Sita, the missing gray-blue cat, also carried time.

As did Rina, the spunky calico.

And there were others.

As the rain fell, they sought shelter inside derelict buildings, under boxes, anywhere that held out the promise of a dry space.

As the rain ceased, they came out.

Some were very attached to their human companions; others were possessed of a preternatural indifference.

Sammy was not eager to leave Carl and Beth. They were, apart from the dimmest memory of his fellow orphan siblings, the only true family he'd known.

It was clear that they loved him.

But it was also clear that they were constantly rebuilding a house that kept disintegrating.

All the cats knew one thing: Every house would soon disintegrate.

They came to their gathering place. It was in a clearing, behind the former chair factory for which the town had once been known. There were shallow rainwater pools in the uneven, warped lot.

Cars splashed by on the road.

The cats gathered around a fire.

They had summoned the fire.

From the fire, they summoned their ancestor.

It was a truly primitive creature, more like a cat's skeleton in the thinnest veneer of skin and fur. To a human, it may have looked like a proto-being, stepping out of a zoological display case to survey a world from which it was removed by about 33 million years.

The cats gathered around were all vessels of time, but not caught up in quibbling about the passing of years.

Houses were disintegrating, and rivers would start to stumble backwards.

Everything would start running backwards.

The clouded air above Collingsville, above what had once been a mid-state industrial hub, grew dense with certainty.

Following their ancestor, the cats tred a narrow, sure path, in the yellowing light.

In Prehistoric Times

I n 1973, Billie Guthert turned nine years old.

She was thin, and her knees were sharp.

Her hair fell flat and straight.

At school, boys laughed at her, even though they mostly ignored girls.

Girls screamed at her for doing or saying the wrong thing.

It was as if all the girls were all crowded onto a flimsy boat, and Billie threatened to capsize it.

She, like they, was curious about makeup, motherhood, babies, or perhaps one day becoming a ballet dancer, a nurse, an astronaut, maybe even a firefighter or a police woman.

But, she was curious about other things.

Like dinosaurs.

She had a field guide about dinosaurs, that her father found at a flea market.

She carried it around with her, everywhere.

Her mother admonished her to stop looking at it except at home.

People would think she didn't want to talk to them,

her mother said.

She couldn't explain to her mother, or anyone, that the field guide was like a sanctuary. It was a sanctuary from all the indignities at school.

Saturday was for television — cartoons and movies. Billie's mother also fretted about this.

Billie didn't understand why. Saturday was her one day to watch television during the day. She loved the Saturday afternoon movie. Her favorite was *One Million Years B.C.*

It was the closest thing to seeing real dinosaurs, which moved stiffly across the screen. No matter.

She loved a cartoon, *Journey to the Lost World*. The lost world brought 20th century people together with cave people. The lost world had dinosaurs.

Billie knew dinosaurs were long gone before people arrived. It didn't bother her. She would have given most anything to be around the same time as dinosaurs.

"What's your favorite dinosaur?" she asked Walter, a boy in her class, at recess.

"Shut up," Walter said, throwing a pencil at her.

The pencil stuck her lightly in the knee before hitting the floor with a snapping sound. She picked it up.

Walter had thrown away a perfectly good pencil, and turned his back to her.

She could have stabbed him in the head with it. But she knew the recess monitor would blame her, and not Walter.

She knew, because this had all happened before, with another boy, Joey, who had thrown a rock at her.

The rock hit her in the eye. She threw it back at Joey,

and ended up writing, "I will not throw rocks" 100 times on a paper that the teacher then ripped up.

Joey was not punished. But, about a week later, he was held in detention, when he managed to get into the teacher's lounge with a marker and scrawl on the door: "Your all pigs."

No one cared that his grammar was bad. His friends were impressed. When he wrote it down for his class-mates, Billie smirked at the incorrect "your," but said nothing.

Billie moved through the school day and recess in the same way, as if through corridors in a dream. Noise around her was blurry and faded.

She tried playing jump rope with some of the girls. A tallish girl named Marie always seemed to be in charge.

She told her mother about the jump rope group, and how she didn't like Marie for being bossy.

"Well, try," her mother had said. "Just do your best."

The next time, at recess, Billie reluctantly came to the jump rope group.

They stared at her, and then looked back at Marie.

"Can I join," she asked.

One girl, Cathy, said, "We're playing 'Queen Bee.' The bee chases the other girl through the rope. If you trip, you're out."

The school play area, like most play areas, was asphalt.

"Okay," Billie said.

Things went fairly well, mostly because no one chose Billie as the queen bee, or as the person to chase. Be-hind her, someone murmured, "Just do it. She'll trip, and then she'll be out."

It hurt, but Billie shrugged it off.

Before she realized what she was saying, Billie asked Marie: "What's your favorite dinosaur."

The rope stopped with a sharp crack.

"Billie," Marie guffawed. "Get serious. No one cares about dinosaurs!"

"I do," Billie said, and walked away.

No one threw anything at her. For Marie and her group, recess time was fleeting, and not to be wasted. The jump rope game had already resumed. The girls chanted, witch-like, "Queen Bee, chasing me, I, choose, Caroline!"

Billie had an older brother, Jeff, 15. Jeff was a kind of weird bridge between her and their parents. Jeff could be alone at home; Billie could not.

Jeff and their parents argued sometimes.

Jeff smoked 'pot.'

Billie wasn't entirely sure what that meant, except that smelled heavy and sweet through his bedroom door.

Jeff had friends. They had long hair and grim faces, as he did.

Some of them had girlfriends. They looked like tall, almost glamorous versions of girls at school, except there was no judgement of her in their eyes.

It was not uncommon for there to be a girl her brother had his arm around.

In another few weeks, that girl would still be there. But, she would file past him with the others, and pass him a stare that would have buckled even the imperious Marie at school.

There was a new girl, Rhonda, with blue eyes, long,

thick eyelashes, super-straight long hair, and an orange top that tied at the neck. Rhonda would say, "Hey Billie, how're you?"

"Fine," Billie would say, but her voice brightened. Rhonda let Billie try on her makeup and even did her hair once.

Rhonda would listen to Billie's stories about dinosaurs.

Billie drew her a picture of a stegosaurus. "I'm going to put this up in my room," Rhonda declared, elated.

Billie never saw Rhonda's room, but she imagined it.

In Billie's vision, Rhonda's room was wonderful, with colored beads dangling in the doorway, and a bed with curtains around it. Her stegosaurus picture was in a frame, on the wall, amid wallpaper roses.

Jeff's room, on the other hand, was an alien, forbidden place with scary rock music and smelly "pot."

One day, Billie found the fortitude to tell Rhonda what the kids at school were like.

Rhonda said, "That stinks. But you know what, you're smart, so just ignore them. They're jealous because they can't read and draw like you."

Billie wasn't sure if that was true. But it made Billie feel better to hear it.

One Saturday afternoon, Billie's parents went out and left Jeff in charge.

They did not care for a lot of what Jeff did, Billie knew.

Still, she would overhear her mother say things like, "I hope Billie grows out of this phase. At least Jeff has friends."

So they went out. Billie was not sure where they went.

Jeff said, "A marriage counselor," and then took to the stairs in loud, heavy footsteps.

Billie was left without any explanation. Her parents were already married. Why they would be seeing a marriage counselor, she wondered. She felt something hot, like flames in her chest and throat.

Before long, some friends of Jeff's were at the back door. They came in without waiting for anyone to let them. They were always a big noisy throng and this time, it was no different.

There were a few girls, but no Rhonda.

This left Billie with a vague sense of anxiety and disappointment.

"Hi, I'm Val," said a girl Billie never saw before.

"Um, hi," Billie managed.

They all went upstairs, and Billie heard Jeff greet them. The door shut emphatically.

Music came on.

Billie could hear the vague, loud sounds. She could hear the laughter.

She could hear the din, even from downstairs. She was still in the kitchen, the back door still slightly ajar.

A terrible realization came to her. She held her favorite plush toy, a stegosaurus.

She thought of this girl, Val, and knew, without anyone telling her, that Rhonda was never coming back.

Tears pooled in her eyes, and her face felt as if burning, like an oncoming fever.

She sat down on a chair at the table, and shuddered as she wept.

She clutched her plush stegosaurus, which collected

up her tears. Not for the first time, but never before with such ferocious grief.

Jeff came downstairs, to the kitchen. He went to the refrigerator, then paused to look at his little sister. "What's your problem," he asked.

Billie looked up at him.

He never so much as asked her about school, other kids, her books, or anything. At nine, she had not much to offer.

He had to watch her, and for Jeff, watching consisted of going upstairs with his friends and closing the door to a room where she was forbidden.

But now, her presence seemed to trouble him. "Stop crying," he said. "Mom and Dad will be home soon, and they will take you for ice cream or something."

Billie felt a chill of foreboding. Her field guide book talked about going extinct. Her hands felt clammy, although her face was still warm.

They were already married but going to a marriage counselor.

Billie did not know how to ask her brother about Mom and Dad.

"Did you make her leave," Billie blurted, sliding off the chair and standing in front of her tall, thin brother.

"What, who," he said.

"Rhonda," she said, with some exasperation.

Jeff turned away. With his back to her, he said, "She's gone. Shut up about it."

He rummaged around the pantry until he found a bag of potato chips. He ripped it open and started eating from it. Without saying anything more, he headed back upstairs.

After a few minutes, Billie decided to go up there, too. She wanted to go into her room and shut the door.

But, she paused. She heard laughter coming from the other side of Jeff's bedroom door.

"Dude, you're mean," someone said.

"She's a pain in the ass," she heard her brother say, with genuine outrage.

More crispy, crunching sound of potato chips. The stench of "pot" escaped from under the door.

Someone, a boy, said, "Oh, dude, my chin is numb."

Billie held the plush stegosaurus close to her.

Her head felt heavy. Finally, she sat on the floor, her head against the door.

There was laughter, music, crunching, talking, some of it muddy and unintelligible.

A girl's voice. Val. "Aw, she's okay."

"Fine," her brother said. "You can have her. Then I get her room."

More laughter, crunching, and — "great, thanks for spilling those."

Another girl's voice. A girl named Wendy. "I hate my older brother."

A round of laughter.

Jeff's voice: "Well, your brother's in jail."

Then, Wendy said, without any laughter. "That's where he belongs."

Another voice spoke, high and slurred. "You told us. Like 50 million times. He stole a car. He was wasted. Kind of dumb to bag a guy who's wasted."

Wendy said, "Yeah, well, that's not all."

No one answered. There was an empty, uncomfortable phrase of music playing, and no other sound, not even potato-chip crunching.

The bed springs whined. Someone was getting up.

Billie tried to leap up. She lurched toward her own bedroom door, across the carpet in the hall, still clutching her stegosaurus.

Jeff's door creaked open.

"What the bleeding fuck is wrong with you," he yelled, his face red and purple.

N'nothing," Billie managed.

"C'mon, she's a little kid," Val's voice said, with some exasperation. There were scattered murmurs of, "yeah, man, she's just your little sister." And some laughter, but it sounded uneasy.

Billie struggled to her feet. Val came forward, and helped her.

Billie made no effort to stop her tears. No one laughed except Robert, the one with the numb chin.

"It's okay," Val said. It wasn't musical, like Rhonda's voice, but it wasn't unkind.

Val caught Billie's hand, and led her to her own room. Once they were inside, Val closed the door with a purposeful shove.

Billie heard some muttering in the hallway. She was sure it was Wendy. "Jeff. You're a fuckin' asshole."

It made Billie giggle, a little.

"Ah, see, you're laughing," Val said, sitting her on the bed, and sitting down beside her.

After a moment, Billie felt her courage return, and she asked. "Do you have a favorite dinosaur?"

Instead of answering right away, Val seemed lost and thoughtful for a moment.

There was a bang on the door. Val ignored it. Billie looked up, but said nothing.

"Maybe they've got better weed in there," Robert, of the numb chin, chuckled.

Finally, Rhonda said, "I don't really know, but I saw a brontosaurus on TV one time, and he seemed okay." The young girl and older girl both smiled at each other.

Another loud knock.

Val stood up. She yelled. "What! Because you're the one who needs a babysitter?"

Then, she said something to Billie that truly startled her. "I like your brother, no offense, but Wendy's right."

Billie finished for her: "He's a fuckin' asshole."

Swearing was more liberating than Billie ever could have imagined.

The following week, the group came, but they were different. Not joking, not really talking much. Music blared, but there was no laughing or comments about numb chins.

There was no Wendy, and there was no Val. In fact, there was only a slight, slender girl, Lisa, with ghostly skin and dark, dark circles around her eyes. She made Billie shiver a little.

In the weeks to come, Jeff was at home less and less frequently.

Billie began to annex his room. Now that she'd seen it, it wasn't so scary.

At first, it was hard. The feral-looking rock stars looked down on her from slightly-bowed posters on the wall.

Pink Floyd, Led Zeppelin, The Who. Alice Cooper, with the strange name, wild eyes set in dark circles.

The images of rock stars menaced and intrigued her in turns. Going in her brother's room was like a little vacation in another land. Plus, it made her feel almost smug.

He couldn't do anything to stop her.

She put some stuffed animals — rabbits, cats with pink ribbons around their necks — on the pillows on his bed.

In the center, she placed the stegosaurus.

If she was sure of anything, it was that Jeff would not be happy to see her stuffed animals, with round eyes and pink ribbons, surrounded by his posters of rock stars.

As she stood very still, surveying the room, she realized something.

Jeff was nine, once, just like her. He was once, three, five, two.

All the rock stars were displayed over wallpaper with old-fashioned-looking fire engines.

In times before Billie was born, in prehistoric times, Jeff had even been a baby once.

"I bet he peed the bed," she said out loud. She only wished Val, or Wendy, or Rhonda, could be there to hear it.

Val, Wendy, Rhonda. They were from the future.

She could be like them, one day. Tall, pretty, and calling people "fucking assholes" when they were, and not ended up having to write a hundred times, "I will not call people fucking assholes."

And, something else. She laid the dinosaur field guide next to her faithful stegosaurus.

Someone had to find out about dinosaurs in order to write that book, or even fashion a template for a stuffed animal.

Another realization. Maybe there was more to learn about them. Maybe she could be the one to learn it, share it. Some day.

Billie knew how to use the record player; her parents had one downstairs.

Billie was allowed to use it. She began to accumulate permission to do many things, such as using the toaster. Supper began to consist more and more of toasted sandwiches she made herself.

Her mother began to work more evenings.

Her father picked up extra hours on his shift, her mother said.

They argued, downstairs.

About him spending all his weekend time at yard sales and not helping in the house.

About her picking at the kids.

"They're kids!" it sounded like an explosion.

Billie, lying on her brother's bed, clutched her stegosaurus more tightly than ever, and opened her field guide to the chapter: How Did The Dinosaurs Go Extinct.

She read, once again, how no one was sure how the dinosaurs finally vanished. There was an illustration of a triceratops, almost skeletal, in the snow.

She conjured an image — her mother and father, first together, then apart, walking in the snow.

Jeff, straight hair around his shoulders, no jacket because he never wore one, even in the winter. He trailed behind his parents, at first, but then drifted off on his own path, over a distant hill.

It did not make her sad. In fact, she found herself summoning tt again and again, looking at the illustration of the foreign triceratops to codify it.

No matter how many times she did this, she did not see herself in it, anywhere.

She lay on Jeff's bed, surrounded by her stuffed animals in a kind of waking dream.

After a while, she got up and began looking in the small mirror above his dresser.

She saw her present self, and a glimpse of her future self, tall, with long hair.

She closed her eyes.

An image came into focus, and she was in it.

She saw a primordial world, with fields of marsh grass, a misty blue sky, and slow, bovine dinosaurs, calling to each other in low tones.

Wasp World

The secret to life is keeping things in order.

At 28, Mark repeated this thought often to himself.

The thought carried him graduate school, and into a successful and adequately challenging career as a financial advisor.

He sometimes wondered at the necessity of such a profession. We live in a country bursting with money, and so many people don't understand it. And thus, my job security, he thought.

Mark kept his life tidy and his finances in check. He took modest vacations, usually camping trips in the White Mountains for extended weekends.

He played tennis with his girlfriend, Jeanne. He was an average player, but so was she. Therefore, no challenge, no threat.

The point was to spend time together — and for Mark, importantly, time not filled up with chatter of no consequence.

But Mark did not lack passion in his life. He had a passion. He had taken a concentrated study in school, in the zoology of invertebrates — but never seriously considered that he could make a living at it.

It was a passion Jeanne respected — her father had been a professor of botany — but she regarded it with some ambivalence. In her opinion, Mark had an articulate mind, and was capable of studying, but not appreciating.

Jeanne enjoyed gardens, both from a scientific perspective inherited from her father, and an aesthetical one. Her mother was a botanical illustrator.

One day, Jeanne suggested she and Mark go to a butterfly park that had recently opened.

It was an airy atrium, filled with light. Plants were meticulously groomed, and soothing, New Age type music was piped in.

The butterflies soared, and fluttered, in dazzling colors.

They rested on leafs, fanning their wings.

There was a man and a woman with a small child. A butterfly alighted on the child's shoulder, and he screamed.

His parents hushed him, and looked around — almost as if they thought the butterflies would not approve.

The butterfly remained fixed on the child's shoulder.

"Don't touch it," the woman pleaded. "You'll hurt it."

A tear streamed down the child's face, the parents took turns calming and admonishing him.

At last the butterfly went off on its own volition. The child was still crying.

Mark and Jeanne looked at each other, in a kind of

shared, telepathic sigh.

"I was never afraid of insects," Jeanne said.

Mark said, "That's not the first time I've seen that. Some people think all insects bite or sting. They instill it in their kids."

Mark's office was located in a suburban park. It was not the modern kind, with a cafeteria and gym.

There was such a park across the way, but it required walking or driving there, and eating up precious break and lunch time.

The office complex huddled near a highway, with a buffer of trees and some wetland between them.

It was part of a strip of offices and light industrial complexes strung along the highway, which stood as a buffer between them and an otherwise quiet and affluent New England town.

A fox emerged from the trees and strolled into the parking lot.

People from Mark's office, the nearby aviation school and even the daycare, came out to inspect it. The fox surveyed them all, then turned and retreated.

She had great, grave, copper eyes.

Some of the gathering simply smiled or tried for a photo. Some said philosophically that there was lots of conservation land around — the townspeople had been eager to preserve all the land they could. So, someone said, expected to see wildlife.

But a few people got on the local police, state police, environmental police, and even a dog grooming business. They also called the building management.

An email memo went around to all the tenants, with

a request that it be shared to all employees and guests. In polite language, it said the fox could not be trapped or moved, and to simply avoid contact with it.

"How are we supposed to do that with these kids?" A woman picking up her child at daycare asked.

Before Mark could stop himself, he said, "Keep an eye on your kids."

The woman looked at him in indignant disbelief. Her son laughed.

Later that night, he told Jeanne when he stopped by her townhouse. It was her night to make dinner.

"Um, Mark, you need a better filter," she said as she opened the oven. She was making a pot roast.

"She's just a concerned mom, that's all."

The conversation changed quickly. Children were not something either of them talked about with any comfort. There had been a similar unease at the butterfly park.

The truth was that Mark had many days, and nights, when he imagined a world without people. People, he decided, couldn't manage money, couldn't manage kids. And they couldn't manage nature. More accurately, they couldn't handle it.

On Facebook, a friend posted a photo of an insect that he found on his car. The caption said simply, "What the actual eff is this." There were comments of shock, amazement and disgust.

Mark knew what it was. It was an enormous wasp, with a magnificent, curled tail. 'It's an ichneumon wasp," he wrote.

There were no more comments after that. It was as

if no one knew what to say, because someone actually knew what this creature was.

At work, Mark stepped outside to make a phone call. He glanced around, but did not see the fox.

He wanted a private space. He went to a tinted-glass tunnel that connected the park's two wings.

When Mark opened the door, and took out his phone, he looked up and realized why the corridor was so quiet.

He heard a scratching sound. There was a loose tile in the ceiling. Darting freely in and out were some paper wasps.

As much as Mark liked and respected insects, he respected the stinging ones enough to keep his distance.

However, as he moved to open the door, he stopped.

The scratching noise mixed with the purposeful hum of their slender wings.

For the first time, perhaps, he appreciated the poetry of what they did, the grace.

Through the displaced tile, he could see just a faint outline of the exquisite honeycomb of their nest.

They paid him no attention. He posed no threat, after all. That was both satisfying, and unnerving. He, the human many times their size, capable of calling an exterminator with a fire bomb, posed no threat.

They seemed to know it. He was sure they did.

After work, Jeanne came over. His turn to cook dinner.

Spaghetti.

It was not lost on her. She made a pot roast; he would boil up spaghetti.

She sat on the couch, peering over the divider that

separated the small living room from the kitchenette.

As he stirred, he wondered if she would get up and help. She would not. It was a quiet protest, and he knew it.

He looked past it and told her about the wasp's nest.

"I'm not really a fan," Jeanne said. "I told you, remember, my mother and father set up bluebird boxes in the marsh."

"Yeah, you said that. It was a good idea," he said, looking at the bubbling water.

"Did you forget what happened, wasps came and killed the baby birds," she said.

"And those butterfly boxes, they build nests in there, too."

"Well, they're very adaptable. Butterfly boxes, office parks."

"I know. I don't know why the shitty species are adaptable and the nice ones aren't. Like starlings. All over the damn place. Knocking out the bluebirds."

"You chose a career in software," he reminded her.

"It makes better money than science," she reminded him. "Like you, right?"

This is the longest-boiling water ever, he thought to himself.

"I think you should tell building management, " she said. "I mean, there's a daycare there, right? Not good having a wasp's nest."

He changed the subject and started talking about her father; they were due to visit her parents soon.

She remarked on the delicious spaghetti; "'very good, for spaghetti" was plain to hear in her voice.

That night, he had a curious dream. He was walking around in the butterfly garden, alone. No disheveled matrons with fearful children. The music was off.

There were no butterflies.

He looked up, just as he had done in the corridor.

Everywhere was a panoply of delicate, paper nests.

They were attached to the roof, to the branches of the decorative trees.

The air thrummed with the sounds of industry, of beating wings.

The slender-waisted bodies gleamed black in the light, as did slick, glassy wings.

Now and then, two would race toward each other, in mid-air, in a dance of combat, almost ritual.

Invariably, one would fall.

Then, two massive clouds sped, blended, in a crash like the cymbals of an orchestra/

It was a ballet of war, an epic war, like that told in the Iliad or the Mahabharata.

Bodies fell, gloriously, like Hector of Troy, or Achilles; great, even in their defeat.

Jeanne had spent the night. But morning brought the work day; she was up, showering briskly, and gone.

That they still kept separate abodes had some purpose. But Mark thought perhaps it was time to begin a transition, to cohabitating. That would make more sense financially, and from a time management standpoint. So far, Jeanne had not raised the idea. Perhaps he should.

Though he wondered why she hadn't.

At lunch, he thought to call her and tell her about his

dream.

He usually called her at lunch.

Today, instead, he took a stroll around the grounds.

The day was warm. May was promising a speedy transition into June, and its heat.

From the daycare — walled like a Persian garden — he could hear sounds. Happy sounds, kid sounds. He peered around the wall.

One child was lining up rotten-looking crab apples in a row.

Another child was arguing with yet another child about the fox. They argued whether it was red or purple, and it was clear neither one of them had seen it.

A little girl had a match. How did she get that, he wondered. She must have sneaked in, like contraband.

In a moment, an aide appeared, and took the match away. She proceeded to confiscate the rotten crab apples, too, and ordered the bickering fox-debaters inside.

"It's time for a snack," she announced nervously.

Mark walked back across the lot. When he was a kid no one cared about playing with matches or crab apples, or the color of foxes. "You can hear the helicopters churning overhead," Jeanne would have said, or words to that effect. Helicopter parents, and in their stead, helicopter aides.

But the matches had gotten past them. Maybe not hovering closely enough.

That evening, as he pulled into the guest section of the parking lot at Jeanne's building, she was already outside, downstairs, a look of consternation on her face.

If this is about the spaghetti, his mind began.

Without saying hello, she said, "Come look."

Her garage door was open. He wasn't sure what he was to look at. She pointed.

"Up there!"

Then, he saw.

A hornet slipped out. "Yeah, they'll do that," he observed.

Her car was not there. "I'm parked in the lot for now. I already called maintenance," she said.

"Maintenance," he repeated.

Their eyes met, and he felt a chill. The chill was what her eyes reflected back at him. He was about to tell her to leave them alone. And she knew it.

She backed two steps away.

After a moment, she said, "You're making dinner. Not spaghetti."

That night, the dream came again.

The atrium now was darker — there were more nests, he realized, casting their shadows on the path, the garden, the walls, like sand dunes at night.

The sounds filled the air, some lower pitched, some higher, like a true symphony. Varied species, in varied sizes, wing spans and velocity.

In that humming air, there were the clashes — only greater now, and a rain of the defeated, falling like an angry rain.

The stakes were too high for anything less.

He awoke. The clock with illuminated numerals said it was just after 4 a.m.

He felt numb. His hands, his arms, seemed void of sensation. Even his face, his eyes. It was as if — as if paralyzed, by stings, by venom.

He inhaled, and even his lungs felt leaden.

Maybe I'm still asleep, he thought, though he knew he was not.

Jeanne, beside him, in a deep, true sleep, sighed in her perfect, dreaming, REM state.

A dream no doubt filled with bluebirds and butterflies. He grimaced.

A few moments later, sleep returned, this time, dreamless.

At 7 a.m., Jeanne rose, and nudged him.

"Sleeping beauty," she said. Even as he struggled for consciousness, the tone in her voice was unmistakable.

He found that he still felt stiff, and immovable. "I feel like crap," he pronounced. "Maybe I have a cold."

She swatted him with a pillow. "Men," she said.

"I'm serious."

"Then call in," she said, already up and grabbing at the outfit she'd laid out the night before.

She disappeared. The hissing sound of the shower came, and the slightest drift of hot steam through the still-open bedroom door.

He grasped at the night table for his phone, nearly dropping it.

After calling, he fell back asleep.

He began to dream.

He was at the atrium, again. Only, the militant sound of humming was gone. There was only a pale, lonely sound of wings scratching.

He looked up at the ceiling, now almost completely obscured. This amplified the silence.

He looked down, at the winding footpath. He could barely see the inlaid bricks.

It was a path of carnage. A wretched, snapping sound — he stepped back.

No use.

They were everywhere, a great, black trail of grief, with occasionally, a buzzing struggle that then stopped. He regarded their empty nests above, and saw the one nest with any suggestion of life.

Bodies darted in and out of it and around it.

Indifference, he realized. They'd won, and so they went back to their daily tasks.

The dream faded in and out like this for hours, in the same cycle.

It was getting dark outside, he saw the greyness descend upon the bedroom.

His heart felt icy in his chest. He moved his left hand stiffly, and then his right.

He moved one foot under the covers, just a brief motion, to the side. He moved the other the same way.

He breathed deeply, and sat up, feeling both relieved and foolish. He was glad Jeanne hadn't seen. Or, perhaps she had, and didn't care.

"What I miss?" he asked his coworker Jonathan.

"What did you miss?" Jonathan leaned back in his chair. "Oh, man. It was like a 70s disaster movie."

"Are you talking about the Herber account?"

Jonathan laughed, and removed his glasses to wipe them.

"That daycare is like Lord of The Flies!"

Mark's knees suddenly felt weak.

"They had a prison break," Jonathan said. "Two of them breached the perimeter."

"It's not funny, Jon," snapped Marlene, from the adjoining cubicle.

Nothing was funny to Marlene. But on this occasion, Mark had a sick feeling that she was right.

"Those kids coulda been hit by a car!"

"They also could have burned the place down," Jon said. "They've got a pyromaniac over there."

The little girl with matches, Mark thought.

"She got into the corridor through the daycare emergency exit, I guess. She had a rolled-up newspaper, with flames on one end and told everyone it was a lightsaber, or something."

Jon was still smiling. Mark noticed a few other people smirking, and others looking Jon's way with disapproval.

"Uh, so, what happened," Mark said, his lower jaw trembling.

"The two little arsonists got a chair, and she climbed on it, and set the ceiling ablaze!" now Jon made no effort at composure, and with near-delirium with laughter. "Oh, man. The fire trucks, the rescue ladder."

Mark felt his face go gray with horror.

"It gets better. Turns out there's a huge wasp nest in there. They closed the daycare the next few days, so they can fumigate!" Jonathan was now dissolved into laughter, as were some others. "Damn good thing," someone said. "I'm allergic to those little bastards."

"What, kids?" someone joshed.

"Yeah, them too."

Marlene glared.

He got up from his desk, and bolted outside.

The corridor was taped up, the glass black with carbon. He stood, and stared, and felt hot tears coursing down his face.

He had failed.

Some higher functioning part of his brain said, time to get back into character.

He turned, reluctantly, to go back inside.

He worked calmly and efficiently through the rest of the day, putting right everything that had fallen into chaos the one day he was out.

At the end of the day, he watched as others went to the cars, and the lot slowly emptied out.

There was one van in the lot. On the side, it said, PESTS 'BEE' GONE.

He knew his next great battle was not to be fought on this front. It was too late.

He went out to the lot, but did not go to his car.

Instead, he walked around the perimeter of the complex, until he came to a patch of trees where he knew a small trail led, as a clandestine shortcut to a nearby corridor of conservation land.

His throat was dry, and flies swiped at his head as he perspired.

His phone vibrated in his pocket. He stopped, and looked passingly at the text message from Jeanne. It said ominously: "We have to talk."

No, we don't, he thought, putting the phone back and shutting it off. Why talk when it was pretty clear. Just saying "We have to talk" said it all.

Let her go back to her butterflies, he thought, and

pressed on, his footfall more forceful.

Before long, he came to a clearing, a meadow with dried, overlong grass. Here and there, a field mouse leapt.

A hawk circled, distantly — a warning, he knew, to other hocks, a signal of territory.

"These are your field mice, we get it," Mark chuckled. His voice sounded not like his own. It sounded strange, almost feral.

The trail divided. One branch, he knew, led to a buffer of marsh around some private property.

The other went toward the conservation land.

He stopped. His heart was like thunder. His feet were pained, in office shoes entirely unsuited for a nature hike

His eyes focused. The air was thick, humid; it hummed with katydids, crickets and frogs, and a mocking bird's litany of foreign songs.

He saw it, then, like a dim cloud over the edge of the rising land. It glinted, like a mythical city.

The clouds rumbled. But there was another sound, a growing hum, pitching high, low.

He left the trail.

He pushed through the grass; a musky fragrance arose in the humidity and heat.

The grass threatened to twine around his legs.

And then, just as surely, he knew, he was glimpsing a place of promise, but would not reach it.

He buckled, fell, the grass folding quickly around him, above him.

His ears filled with the rushing sound.

He closed his eyes, and saw the dream.

The atrium, darkened with silent nests above.

Like a fleet of dark angels, they came, to the footpath that had become a grave of their fallen enemies.

Streamlined wings and black bodies glinted faintly; the path appeared to be covered with brilliant, black, smooth pebbles, spread unevenly.

The inert bodies began to rise, in the clutches of their conquerors, and the host ascended, in the unified hum of the wings of both living and dead.

This was their heaven, and in nature's heaven, nothing went to waste.

A glorious cycle would soon begin again.

He exhaled into the warm, sweet, dry grass.

•••

Donald Winston and his sister, Laura Winston Barnes, had grown up in comfort, protected from the uncertainty of survival by their family's wealth.

They had, however, grown up without much tranquility in their upstanding home in this New England town.

It was a town filled with graceful homes, the burying grounds of Revolutionary War heroes — and families whose names could be found on the roster of the Mayflower.

As adults, Donald and Laura had not seen it much.

Donald had lobbied for and won a job transfer to an office in Minneapolis.

Laura had finished her graduate studies and opted for a teaching position in Santa Fe, declaring the mountains, the dry air and the culture to be a balm for her spirit.

Donald knew his sister was not so much healed as

covering the same pain as he.

Both had chosen to place their careers and lives a good distance from their parents.

Hartwell Winston was the scion of a textile family and had a knack for real estate. He was also what Donald and Laura as adults would describe bitterly as a "functioning alcoholic."

He could deftly attend to business — with no small help from the fleet of associates he hired — and speak eloquently at civic club meetings, the opening of a new playground and the dedication of a conservation park.

He was also lauded for his efforts to preserve open space. The community praised itself for an inherited, collective affluence — nay, wisdom — allowing the purchase and protection of forest and fields.

Such measures always passed at Town Meeting, and spared these lands from the banal-looking developments springing up in neighboring, less prudent towns.

Hartwell Winston often led the charge, speaking grandly during the discussion periods of Town Meeting, which he faithfully attended.

When he arrived home, the functioning ended and the long descent into the drink-driven cruelties began, directed at his son, daughter and on occasion, his wife, their mother, Elizabeth Langsham Winston.

She did what neither children had the freedom to do. She excused herself from her husband's wrath for lengthy periods, seeking respite at MacLean Hospital or one of a network of private drug and alcohol rehabilitation centers.

She was praised quietly by her small circle of intimate

friends for having the courage — and the means — to do so.

From their far-flung spheres in Minneapolis and Santa Fe, their now-grown children did not visit, even for holidays or birthdays.

They sent notes of apologies in response to invitations for family weddings or christenings, usually accompanied by respectably large checks as gifts.

They maintained the legal, necessary discourse with their parents through their attorneys.

These attorneys duly notified them as instructed when Hartwell Winston died of a heart attack in his study, followed weeks later by their mother. She succumbed to an infection from a hypodermic needle.

A funeral home that had serviced the family with efficiency and discretion for generations released obituaries to the local newspaper, with "died at home" and "died of a brief illness."

Letters of gratitude and condolence filled the same editions of that newspaper, detailing the couple's achievements, generosity and active role in town government.

Donald and Laura flew in, each with their spouses and very young children. Everyone had been briefed on how to act, and what to say.

The calling hours, service in the sparse, light-filled Methodist church, and burials went just as they should.

Requesting and receiving time to "grieve in private," they met with the executor and their attorneys.

Meanwhile, at a Colonial Heritage Society meeting at the historic Pendleton Inn, the chairman said, "Well, with Harty gone, someone has to take over the cognac."

A pent-up, hearty laughter rang out from everyone at the table.

The Winstons would not forget their children's silence and, as they saw it, lack of gratitude. They left a large sum to the town's conservation fund; attorneys filed the paperwork to contest the will.

Apart from the Winstons' residence and adjoining land, the only asset left to them outright was a farm.

It had once been a working farm, dating back almost to the times that colonists clear-cut the forest to extract sustenance from the unyielding New England soil.

Of late, it was a farm in name only; with a feral apple orchard, a green house in disrepair, and a barn that, for all its great past, would likely face demolition.

The siblings wanted to sell the property, totaling about 10 or so acres; it bordered the Spring Well Conservation Sanctuary, and they could have put it into a protective agricultural trust.

Certainly, many were already urging them to do so. They heard pleas, again and again — the town is changing. It had been changing since the 1950s when the state laid down a four-lane highway, rudely cutting the town in half.

There were poorly-planned office parks and even a shoddy-looking affordable housing complex. It seemed the elders were facing a stark reality. In modern economic times, the new generation did not always see the good fortune of their predecessors.

Land came at a tremendous premium, and its sale could keep a family solvent, if needs must.

The attorneys weighed in. First things first, they admonished.

Donald and Laura set an appointment.

They walked with the town conservation agent and an independent environmental consultant, to survey the land.

The orchard trees looked withered and sad.

Honey bees darted about, and then strangely, parted and flew away as if into space.

Brother and sister looked at each other quizzically for a moment. The conservation agent felt his hands grow cold.

"Sweet, bleeding —" the consultant jumped back and nearly fell, looking ragged and crooked, almost comical, like a scarecrow that fell from its post.

They all looked down.

"It's him," the conservation agent said. "Holy God."

Laura fell against her brother before righting herself.

A cross was spread out in the grass, of tattered clothing that flickered in the warm breeze.

A startled cloud of wasps flew up; one glanced at the conservation agent's arm and he yelled.

A few wasps still moved tenaciously, on a crest of white framed with what appeared to be the remainder of a shirt collar.

No one had to say out loud what it was.

Laura covered her face with her hands.

None of them realized it, but they were all weeping.

Laura finally fumbled at her cell phone to call the police.

The conservation agent gained some measure of composure. "This — there was someone missing," he stammered. "His car was at work. His girlfriend — the chief had a press release."

No one was listening to him.

Donald's chest heaved, his stomach roiled; he fought to stay calm. Ridiculously, he saw his father laid out, meticulous, in his flower-lined casket.

There was no order or ceremony here. Nature's heaven, he thought absurdly.

The air hummed; the din grew in volume.

Laura could no longer stand to keep looking.

She looked up, at the green house. One of her father's failed, drink-fueled experiments.

It would have been a great, wondrous botanical sanctuary.

The inside was darkened; a glass pane was broken.

It had become a sanctuary, but not for plants.

Her lower jaw quaked. She dropped her phone; it vanished in the grass.

Dark clouds gathered in the sky, promising rain.

A darker cloud was pooling through the broken glass, in a great black wave of purpose.

The Living with Zombies Support Group

The August evening air was damp and uncomfortable.

Paula's skin felt clammy, but it was too warm for a sweater.

There was a note on the front door of the Clark Middle School: "SG Please use the side door."

The side door was unlocked, which also made her uncomfortable.

Inside was the school gym, where a summer camp was meeting, echoing with screeches, laughter and a thumping basketball. It was exuberant enough to seem incongruous.

Then, a door with another note: "SG Welcome."

About a half dozen men and women sat in cramped-looking chairs arranged in a half circle.

The smell of coffee was the first welcome moment all day.

Everyone turned and half-smiled as she sat down.

A man in a checked shirt, slightly heavy set, with a buzz cut and a longish, uneven beard, greeted her. "We're just getting started," he said. "Charles, continue your story."

Charles looked tired. They all did. Charles said, "It's hard for men to talk but I think it's important. I feel guilty all the time."

"What makes you feel guilty," the moderator asked.

"Anyone mind if I swear?" Then, "Because I want to rip their fucking arms off." One woman sucked in her breath. A few others nodded understandingly.

Paula blurted: "Me, too."

The moderator said: "Oh, man, sorry. Everyone this is our new member, um"

"Paula. Hi everyone."

A few people muttered, Hi. The man who had been talking stared downward slightly, with reddened eyes.

The moderator: "So, like just a few rules. Don't repeat stuff said here, and no cross-talking."

Paula pursed her lips, annoyed at being told about a rule she had already broken.

But she was pretty sure everyone in there wanted to do what Charles said: Rip their fucking arms off.

The tale of the twins

More than once Paula thought about selling the house and moving herself and Lydia to the city. Museums and stores within walking distance.

But it would be hard on a girl of only 13. Especially one who'd just lost her father. Well not just. Two years.

Lydia didn't act out the way Paula had heard kids who lost a parent might. In some ways Lydia's reaction bothered her more. Lydia became slow, quiet, deliberate in everything. She paused greatly before speaking or doing anything.

Paula felt as if watching a fire from a careless match catch furtively at leaves on a forest floor. As if the worst would come, with no warning.

They knew of only one other family that had lost a parent. The Keppers. They had fraternal twins, Kendra and James. They were Lydia's age, and Kendra was in Lydia's homeroom.

On Christmas Day, the Kepper twins were nowhere to be found. Naturally, nowadays, everyone feared the worst.

It turned out they had joined some slightly-older kids taking bricks to the Clark Middle School windows.

Lydia had dismissed them before that from her small, fragile circle of friends. After the school incident, Paula felt relieved.

In the parking lot of the school once more, Paula glanced for a moment at the panes in the window that outshone the others.

She guessed that these were the ones the schools replaced following the Christmas Day vandalism spree.

Their parents thought those kids were 'taken,' Paula thought. 'I bet they wish they had been.' She regretted even the thought, and resolved not to bring it to the group.

Bitchy in widowhood

At the next meeting, someone had brought anisette cookies to share.

Paula assumed it was the woman with the slightly-green hair, wearing a pink, jeweled sweater. She had anisette freak written all over her, somehow.

But that woman said, "Thanks for the cookies, Charles. I didn't know you were quite the chef!"

Paula felt her lips go thin and pursed.

"Hey no problem," said Charles. It was the same Charles who last week declared he wanted to "rip their fucking arms off."

"Well, I guess we're a group of many talents," Paula heard herself say out loud, in a not-so-loud voice.

The others looked at her quizzically as she sat down. The jewel sweater lady blinked.

More muted laughter, some of it uncomfortable.

The moderator had made some effort to trim his beard.

He had told them all last week of his master's degree in psychology, and that he played part-time in a thrash metal band. To relieve tension, he said. It's a tense time.

"So I thought we'd start tonight's meeting, by talking about fear. Pam, you wanna go first?"

Pam was the gem-sweater lady. "Well, I think we're all a little afraid," she offered.

That's helpful, Paula thought. Then: I really am getting bitchy. Does widowhood make you bitchy? Maybe I need a cookie.

Meditation in gray

"So....tell me..." Barbara said, almost coyly, when they met for coffee. Paula was thinking it was time they picked a different coffee shop.

Belinda's Stop And Chat was full of quaintness, but the cafe-style tables made her nervous, so close to the delicate displays of cake toppers and china tea sets.

The commuter train would rumble through, and everything would klink slightly.

But the Stop And Chat was near Barbara's studio, in the new co-op where she was a resident artist.

"Well?" Barbara's eyes were girlishly mischievous.

"No, I didn't ask him."

Barbara's shoulders slumped, and her purple artist's smock shifted. "Well, I guess you will know when the time is right."

After a moment, Paula said, "I don't think that's why I'm going." Then: "I know everyone thinks that. It's a support group, not a dating site."

"Well, I'm not going to say whether you should, or shouldn't. I'm just saying, if you think you want to, don't let the setting stop you."

"All he wants to do is rip their arms off," Paula said.

Barbara took her classic, philosophical stance.

"I think a lot of people feel that way. Of course, it's not an answer, but I think he's saying what a lot of people feel."

Paula found herself clutching at her iced tea and sipping at it with a strange, primitive fury.

She and Barbara had been friends since high school, occasionally separated by distance and life circumstance, but always circling back, despite their differences.

Paula saw, clearly, one big difference. Barbara could afford to be philosophical about everything. She worked full-time in her studio because her husband's high-tech job allowed that.

Barbara's hair was going softly gray. Paula knew Barbara and some other women they knew were doing that — to show they weren't afraid of aging.

Paula kept coloring her hair rust-red. Age was not something she frequently discussed; after losing Jack, she felt even more guarded. At work, gray-haired women had a way of turning invisible, as if people thought they could walk right through them.

Paula had never harbored resentment about Barbara, pursuing her lifelong dream of art, dispensing wisdom and wearing loose purple smocks. But now, she knew, her smile was forced.

As a licensed practical nurse, and in her life with Jack, she'd been satisfied. Now, two years after Jack's death, that life seemed almost like watching a movie of someone else's.

"I know you get a lot of people," Barbara said. "They're saying, 'start dating,' blah blah blah.' Only you can decide your path."

Paula smiled again, thinking, she's talking about widowhood like it's an elective class. Then, a hot stab of guilt in her gut. Barbara did care. She always did.

The tremor of dreams

When she was about 10, Paula remembered being awakened in the night by a tremor. It felt like a large truck rumbling down the street.

That was the sound outside tonight, intermittent, sometimes just a soft rumble, sometimes loud, like that long-ago tremor.

The emergency management warnings all said — Don't move. Shelter in place.

Paula thought, I'm alone in this big stupid bed. My daughter's asleep down the hall. If they come here, I'm not sheltering in place. I'll — rip their arms off?

She had taken a cast-iron skillet from the pantry and tucked it under her side of the bed. It seemed comical, but if she had to go down, she would take at least one of them with her.

Through the slightly-open bedroom door, Paula saw a light go on. Just Lydia, probably going to the bathroom.

But Paula got up.

It was Lydia, but she was in the living room, reading. "Oh, honey, did the sound wake you?"

Lydia looked at her mother, confused. "I didn't hear anything." Lying, she's taken to lying. She's a passive-aggressive griever, Paula thought. She suddenly felt as if she was back in the support group thinking of words like, passive-aggressive.

Paula had to get up in four hours and was in no mood or stamina for arguing with her 13-year-old daughter. "Honey, I'm glad you didn't hear anything. But I need you to go to bed." Then, Paula said, "You read a little while longer in your room. It might help make you tired."

At least she reads, Paula told herself. She was pretty sure the Kepper twins did not.

Lydia flashed her a look of half-despair, and slid off the chair. It had been Jack's favorite chair. Lydia often sat there, and Paula didn't fight her on that, either.

Songs in autumn

Summer evaporated as it always did. The leaves were already flashing gold and scarlet.

The school year began, and Lydia was now in the final year of middle school. She approached that milestone with the same vague indifference she did a lot of things these days.

If motherhood had taught Paula anything, it was how to pick battles. If widowhood taught her anything, it was saving her strength for the war.

Everyone was doing that in a way.

The support group continued, meeting each week, in the same room, only now the halls were considerably noisier. Band practice met in the nearby music room, with awkward-sounding french horn and trombone.

A drama club meeting took place. A shrill, crackling voice yelled, "I am innocent of a witch!"

One week, an email went out. The moderator's signature had a little drummer boy icon. "Sorry, everyone, no group meeting tonight, school will be in lock-down. It's just a test, so no worries."

The kids were also accustomed to warnings. Lydia would come home and announce, "We had a drill."

"And, how was that?" With motherhood came the realization that adults forget how to talk to a kid, despite having been one.

Lydia sighed and put her lunch box down on the kitchen table, regarding it strangely.

"Well mom it's kind of the same every time. They make us line up."

"I know it's hard, but they want you all to be safe. I know it must be scary, sometimes."

"The grownups look more scared." Paula sensed, then knew — that was no lie. Lydia was telling the truth.

Then, with a look of near-contempt: "Jimmy Kepper got a suspension."

"What now?"

"He brought a hammer to school," Lydia said. There was a strained effort in her face that made Paula think she was trying not to laugh.

"He said they'd rather fight 'em than line up," Lydia added.

For the first time in more than two years, mother and daughter laughed together, a little.

Later, she thought: the Kepper kids will survive all this because they're not afraid to swing a hammer.

She gave Lydia a frying pan and told her to keep it under the bed. "I have grandma's skillet. I want you to keep this."

"Just in case," Lydia finished for her.

"Exactly. I'm always here for you, you know. But, just in case."

"I don't like Mark."

"Sorry, honey?" It took a full second to realize Lydia was talking about a boy in school, completely changing the subject.

"Lydia I need you to focus."

"Mom, it's good, really. I'm glad. I'll keep it in my room. Mark is in my class. He asked me to the Harvest Home dance."

Paula felt some rare levity. "Well, if you don't want to

go with him, just say so, but be polite. If you just want to go and meet your friends, you know you can."

"Can I think about it?"

"Of course, sweetheart. But the dance is next week, so if you really don't want to go with Mark, you should tell him. In case he wants to ask someone else."

Is everyone living life like this now, or is it just me, Paula wondered. Be ready in case we're attacked. Get ready for the school dance.

In praise of good kids

She shared the story with Charles. Charles was not a Tea And Chat person. Charles liked Roast Beef Wrangler, and Paula felt strangely refreshed.

There was a slight gap in the door, and cool autumn air whistled in.

"She sounds like a good kid," Charles said. Charles was divorced. He had an 18-year-old son, David, working at a grocery store and saving for college.

Charles wasn't divorced in the strictest sense. It all came out at the support group one night: his wife, Ella, had been gardening, late on a spring afternoon.

Then, they appeared in a shadowy host, out of the conversation land that was the reason she had talked them into buying that house in the first place.

Ella did not scream. She did not run.

As Charles told it, she simply got up, brushed the soil off her ripped jeans — from what Paula gathered, Ella was proud of her jean-friendly figure.

Still wearing her gardening gloves,Charles said, Ella walked toward them. They didn't move, or do anything.

One of them put an arm around her back, and they all vanished into the woods.

Charles didn't run after her. He was too angry at that time. Now, he lived in a cloak of guilt.

Paula surmised that this is why he always talked about ripping their arms off.

Barbara was beaming. "I just want what makes you happy," she said, wearing a purple smock with cloth posies on it.

She had sewn them on herself. "If you found someone to hang out with, that's great. Sounds like you both have some things in common."

"We have the same thing everyone has in common," Paula said. "We're scared. But we can't show the kids."

Barbara said, "You have to do what you think is right."

Comforts

Charles liked roast beef and football and was upset when games were delayed because of "drills."

"Drills" and "lockdown" were more than annoyances. They were a reminder of his wife's leaving, which Paula couldn't figure out if it was abduction, or betrayal. Or both.

Who gets up and leaves a good home and a good marriage, for....them?

Barbara was genuinely happy for her, she knew.

Paula felt it was more or less inevitable. Two single parents, meeting week after week in a support group about the same topic (one person made a joke about wrapping his front door with tin foil as a deterrent.)

To which the moderator gave another rule. "Um okay

some people might find that funny but we're here to give practical advice."

Not so cool for a heavy metal drummer, Paula thought.

Charles and Paula talked about it later, at Roast Beef Wrangler.

"Mister Moderator seems a little uptight," Paula said.

Some teens, looking not much older than their own kids, were bunched together in the next booth. A kid guffawed and spattered chocolate milk all over the girl next to him.

She picked up a glass of water, poured it on his head, and stalked off. All his other friends seemed too scared to laugh.

"I can't say I'm looking forward to those days," Paula said. She told of the young man Mark who invited Lydia to the Harvest Home Dance, now just two nights away.

"She told me she didn't want to go with him but then last night, she told me, yes," Paula said.

Charles said. "I can drive 'em there. And, you know, keep an eye on things."

"That would be fine," Paula said.

"We can get something to eat and then go get them from the dance," Charles said.

"That works," Paula said prosaically. Their whole relationship had settled quickly into a prosaic groove. It was the first comfort Paula had felt in a long time.

As they left, they saw a man sitting on the sidewalk. Grumpers. Paula remembered that the kids all called him Grumpers. He was sitting on a towel, and playing a harmonica.

There was a little change in a coffee tin next to him. Paula gave him a dollar. Charles gave him a five dollar bill, and a pair of sunglasses in his jacket.

"Thanks, Man, and Lady," Grumpers said, and went back to the strange, Delphic stream of talk only Grumpers understood.

The reckoning of cold weather

By the night of the dance, the air was chilly.

People walked about in a spirit of apprehension.

Paula felt it too but wasn't sure why, exactly. When the cold weather comes, there is a good chance they will just hibernate. No one will be killed, and no one will leave their spouse and walk off into the woods.

When Lydia came home from school, her face was in a tight glare. She fixed that glare on Charles, who was examining the screens on their porch.

At least we got to keep the house, Paula thought fleetingly.

Then, "Honey, is something wrong?"

"We had another drill today," Lydia said.

Before either of the adults could answer, Lydia said, in a startlingly loud voice: "It's so stupid!"

Charles ventured to say something and then stopped.

Paula said, "Oh, honey I know it's annoying —"

"Mom, it's more than annoying. It's stupid. They aren't there. Nothing's there!"

"Watch your tone," Paula said. "Your going to the dance is conditional upon you being civil." She felt a beam of pride in picking out "good" parenting words.

"I'm sorry," Lydia said. "It's just..."

"I'm gonna go outside and check on the car," Charles said, and slipped out.

Paula half-wished he'd stay.

Even though she knew he was trying to give them space.

"What is it, honey, you can tell me," Paula said, trying not to sound pleading.

"They're not real," Lydia said.

"I wish that were true."

"Miss Abeneth, in social studies," Lydia said. "She told us, to think for ourselves."

"That's important. It's also important to be civil." The great voice of parenting wisdom left as quickly as it had come.

The apparition, the sun

Drop-off at the dance went as planned. Then, Paula and Charles went to the Roast Beef Wrangler.

Paula wrestled with being upset that he stepped out. Rationally, she understood. The aggrieved, widowed mom in her still resented it.

As she got ready, a strange memory came to her. Of being a child. About Lydia's age. She had been raised Catholic, and had insisted on Last Rites for Jack.

In Sunday School class, there was a discussion about Our Lady of Fatima. How in 1917, one day hundreds of people claimed to see the sun, dancing.

But people in a nearby city didn't see the sun move at all.

"People see what they want to see," Jack had once said, in argument she could no longer remember.

Lydia. Lydia's shutting it all down. It's too much. Losing her Dad, and dealing with this menace. It was a terrible revelation, but it made perfect sense. Jack hadn't walked off into the woods, he hadn't been taken by anything except cancer.

Guilt, and more guilt. How they waited so long for testing. How he wouldn't stop working because he said they couldn't afford that.

We just denied it all, and we saw what we wanted to see. Somehow working as a nurse didn't bring any insight to bear. We told ourselves, there's nothing to worry about, Paula felt a knot of pain in her stomach.

After some silence, she spoke.

"In a way, we're still strangers," Paula said, feeling another twinge from childhood — the confessional. The priest had been kind and assured her comic books weren't a sin, unless her parents told her to turn off the light and stop reading.

"Uh, today, with Lydia. You know —I woulda stayed, but, you know, it's you and her. Dad always said don't get in between a fight with two women." His eyes glinted a little.

Paula sighed deeply and nodded. "I keep telling myself I'm not afraid. But I must be. I mean, we all must be or we wouldn't be in that group."

"I just went because I thought it was a different group. You know, like —"

"— Like the movies? A zombie apocalypse?"

"Something like that. I didn't know they were all cry babies."

"They're scared," Paula reiterated.

"I didn't follow her," Charles said. "Ella, I mean. Maybe I shoulda. I think she wanted to leave anyway."

"Well, that was kind of an extreme way to do it," Paula said, then regretted it. She didn't want to pass judgement on his ex. Even if his ex left in a drove of the living dead.

Like a thunder crack

At 10 p.m. Charles went as promised to pick up the kids.

She stood alone on the porch. Moonlight fell thinly through the trees.

She'd intended to use the time paying bills. She had gotten to most, then realized the gas bill was missing. Widow's brain, she sighed inwardly. That's what Barbara had called it.

It was a mundane thing. Paying bills.

The moderator had said something about people getting so comfortable, so used to the situation, of them being all around.

Then, like a crack of thunder, something would happen. A report of a missing adult, or child, even if that same adult or child came home safely.

People began to change their ways. No more trail hikes. No more camping. Bars cleared out well before closing. The streets were silent.

Paula felt suddenly and profoundly angry. Angry that this unbidden plague was changing all their lives.

Anger had worn at her, like a drop of water beating at a stone, slowly, silently. Since the diagnosis. Since being left alone. Since nearly losing their home.

Anger at Barbara, in a world that Paula never had an

issue with but which now seemed dreamlike and pre-posterous.

Barbara in her purple smocks, painting her abstract flowers series. Declaring, "If they come, they come. There's no harm in painting until that time."

Lydia, preadolescent rage threatening to break through, bringing with it all the wrath of a girl facing life without a father.

That wrath threatening the harmony Paula was start-ing to nurture in a relationship of her own.

Smoke to the moon and stars

Paula, who hadn't smoked since she was a high school senior, felt an urge for a cigarette.

Charles smoked. She refused to let him smoke in the house. But he left a pack on the table. She went in, lit a cigarette on the stove burner, and stood outside, feeling grimly triumphant.

She blew the smoke up at the indifferent moon and stars.

The trees rustled; at first, she thought it was the wind.

Then the shadow materialized on the path to the door.

The path she wanted to fix, but couldn't afford to; one job that just didn't make the cut for the limited life in-surance benefits.

Paula coughed dryly. She had rehearsed this mo-ment, as surely everyone had, in her mind. Even in the support group, there had been role-playing exercises.

Her will to battle momentarily flagged. Then, the an-ger flared again.

The shadow advanced. The trees rustled.

"Fucking coward," she said into the cold air.

A voice babbled, like a strange mashup of wasps and crickets trying to outdo each other. Raspy, insect-like.

Her knees felt as if on fire.

Her skillet was uselessly under the bed, inside the house.

But, she had a cigarette.

She went down the steps, slightly dizzy. The nicotine.

More gurgling, more rustling from the trees.

She had not turned on the porch light on because even now it could attract insects. But she wasn't going to turn her back.

"Be strong," the moderator had said.

"You're on my fucking property," Paula said.

The shadowy being shuffled, and muttered.

She rushed, half-blind, and jabbed the cigarette deeply into a face that felt strangely soft, if cold.

The moan of pain shocked her. She staggered, and they both fell, pathetically, onto the grass.

She felt a cold wrist grab at her. The trees seemed to be shouting and the wind howled, all a useless Greek chorus.

For the first time, Paula felt panic. With her free hand she flailed around in the wet grass. A stone slab from the path dislodged.

She took it, shakily, intending to bring it down squarely on the head. Instead, it caught something — maybe the side of the skull — with a sickening crack.

Another moan, and cold, dark trickling, surely blood, from a parched, gaping mouth. Then, a sound almost like weeping.

The trees sighed.

Paula sat up, drenched in sweat, her teeth chattering.

She had always imagined this moment, and here it was, quick, and pathetic. No angry tribe came charging through the trees to take revenge, or even escort her off into the woods, as with Ella.

There was another moan, a tattered chest, heaving, then slowing.

As if someone abruptly changed a channel, she heard a voice, Lydia's voice. "'Cause they're not real!"

A car was pulling in the driveway.

Light splashed across her face. She squinted.

It had actually been there a few minutes, she realized.

Doors slammed.

There was another light. Charles was holding his cell phone down on her, and the prone, ragged figure on the path.

Paula gasped, and no words came out.

Lydia was there beside her, whimpering, heaving — "Oh, mom, God —"

Charles held the cell phone light up.

"Oh, my Jesus," he gasped. Lydia gave a sharp cry.

Lydia was crying. So was Charles.

It was Paula who broke the silence. "Grumpers."

Charles' sunglasses fell from a pocket in the man's grimy shirt, along with a filmy envelope.

The light picked just enough for Paula to realize — her gas bill. It must have fallen from her pocket book when they gave Grumpers the money.

Her head reeled. Grumpers had read the address and

came to give it to her.

The night froze, as they sat in a circle around him.

Grumpers' left cheek scarred with a hideous burn from the cigarette, the right side of his head now like a slope of granite, and moonlight flickering at it, as if on a brook.

Charles punched at his phone, and called the police.

Forgetting, remembering

She wasn't charged. It was considered self-defense. Still, some people in the supermarket and at the school seemed to regard her more coolly.

Something else happened. The support group was cancelled. The drills stopped.

People went out at night.

Charles received a call from his wife. She felt embarrassed, and foolish, she said, but she'd met someone. She agreed to an attorney to sort out child support.

Charles told Paula he had a mind to tell his wife to forget it. But he wanted to make sure their son had some kind of bond with her.

Barbara remained a loyal friend.

"Well, things have changed a lot,"Barbara said in an uncharacteristically pedestrian way.

"I think people won't even talk to me." Paula realized that it wasn't because of the tragic death of a homeless man. It was because he took with him the whole stupid illusion.

Lydia had been right.

Barbara's eyes lit with slight surprise when Paula said: "Maybe in another place, the sun really danced."

Pure

The food was the first thing to go.

The cabinets, the refrigerator, even the glove compartment, where Jessie used to keep candy bars in the event of a long road trip; all bereft now, and soon the cockroaches gave up and vacated.

Jessie made this great purge one night, while insomnia throttled her and she realized what she should have accepted weeks ago.

She simply wasn't going to eat anymore, and no use pretending she was.

Of course, Ricky urged her to go to the doctor, but it was no longer sweet that he cared. It was just irritating. Jessie knew that he sometimes listened outside the door when she went to the bathroom, to make sure she wasn't going to force herself to retch.

"Everything makes me nauseous," she told him. "So forget it, all right?"

Naturally, it was preposterous to think that he would. But Jessie was at a loss to explain the abstinence to herself, let alone him.

She had become resigned to it, being fundamentally

non confrontational anyway, and preferred not to debate it again and again.

A week or so after the food went away, the cigarettes followed, after years of stubbing them out defiantly, only to crawl back to them the next morning, in near-fevered hysteria.

One day, she just couldn't stand to think of black mucus like burgeoning storm clouds, gathering in her lungs and trachea.

As with the food, the departure wasn't really quitting. The need was simply gone, and left no fractured nerves in its place.

Jessie tossed away her ashtrays — the chunky glass one her mother, also a smoker, had given her, and the hideous ceramic alligator one that Ricky had brought back to her from South Carolina. Imagine, using a reptile, of all things, to enable her addiction.

At work, the changes brought applause, and an envy that incited snide comments as soon as she left the break room at the hospital, where she was an assistant radiology technician.

The comfort and rush that food and cigarettes once were brought was replaced by something unexpected — a delight in ordinary things. Ridiculous things. Work itself, and the filmy pictures of X-rays, displayed on light boards for inspection.

She had never found them remotely beautiful, but somehow, now they were. Here was Mrs. Angela Barrington's upper GI. Her ribcage, whispy and fairly-like, Jacob's ladder.

When Ted, the chief technician, stepped out of the

room, she held up her own hand to the spooky light, straining for a glimpse of her own infrastructure. Not yet. She was losing weight, of course, but not with the tragic hurry of an anorexic. Instead, it receded slowly and elegantly, in an easy tide.

Whatever Ricky thought of her peculiarities, he did not deny that she was looking better these days. Smaller, translucent. And her moods, which to him required some kind of barometer to monitor, were now stable, and solid as Mount Everest.

As long as he didn't bring up the taboo subjects of the kitchen and the ashtrays.

When he arrived home, it was to a woman who was not lacking in other appetites.

For a while.

Finally, Jessie awoke one morning positively suffocated by his body, huge and mammalian, like a great, blubbery bear in hibernation.

He was actually only medium in build, although a little paunchy in the front. He was also on the other side of the big bed. Yet he might have been an army regiment, camped on top of her. She flung off the sheets, and ran to the bathroom.

She saw herself in the mirror on the door, and was struck by how comical her form had become to her in the passage of one moist, and exhausting night.

Her breasts were like sacks of meal, her hips like an opening sinkhole. And, she was dry, drier than the Badlands.

With one, icy finger, she made an investigation. She had retracted into herself, and there was no cajoling any glistening warmth from there.

At first, Jesse once again avoided the whole matter altogether. She let Ricky prod and probe as he always had, but she knew she shouldn't underestimate him. He was hardly an oaf. When not even his own touch or saliva could bring her to boiling, he became agitated.

"You shouldn't do this if you really don't want it," he whispered one night.

"What makes you think that?" she whispered back, and instantly regretted it.

"Oh, come on! Don't think I haven't taken the trouble to learn a thing or two about you in the past three years!"

Would he retreat in a huff to the other side, and curl up, like a pupa? She almost hoped he would.

When he seemed asleep, his breath fitful and full of stops and starts like a troubled engine, she got up.

For want of knowing what else to do, she went to the living room, hoping to find a book on her shelf that would provide a moment's distraction.

Jessie found nothing remotely comforting among the sloppy heaps of novels and old college textbooks. She resorted to the bottom shelf, where she kept a handful of children's books that she hadn't been able to part with.

A collection of Edward Lear stories. Too strange. Grimm's Fairy Tales. Too damned morbid. There was a book from her junior high school, tomboy days, days of breaking open milkweed pods, of making caterpillar condos out of milk cartons.

The book was a field guide to reptiles and amphibians.

It had been years since she had even been to a zoo to see snakes snoozing in their glass terrariums, much less gone snooping in the dirt or in a pond for any such creature.

But somehow, the well-thumbed pages were bland and soothing enough, probably because they spoke of a time long before her current problems.

Before she thought much about cigarettes, boys or her weight.

She cocooned under the afghan on the couch to enjoy a reunion with her old friends. The hog-nosed snake, foraging with its upturned snout for toads. The Gila monster, like a badly-made Mexican souvenir purse. The blind salamander in the caves of the Ozarks.

It stunned her, with its fragile beauty against the darkness, so much like the now-beatific X-ray photos at work.

The salamander's skin was so milky and pure that porcelain bones and the slender strands of vein and heart could be clearly seen.

Night's damp warmth assailed her. She felt dirty, coated. She put the book down and went to the bathroom, and started the tub.

When it was ready, she got in, not bothering to get a towel or to turn on the light. She found the vague glow of streetlights through the high, small window to be enough.

She regarded her nebulous form beneath the darkened water, and closed her eyes.

She longed for something she had been working at, or rather, that her body, independent of her, had been working at — a kind of cleanliness she didn't really understand, and at first, hadn't completely wanted.

But, she could admit to herself, alone in the nighttime bath, that it was all somehow all right.

She didn't miss food. She didn't miss cigarettes. She didn't miss Ricky, spasming inside her, rivulets of his sweat seeping into her own pores. She gladly relinquished whatever impurities remained into the bath water.

She thought again of the little salamander, its world so fine, so minimal. It didn't see anything, because it didn't need to. It didn't harbor opaque fat, because it didn't need that, either.

The water and the steam of the sleepless night were making her positively tipsy. Was she so prone to intoxication, having not even had a sip of beer in at least two months?

She yawned and lifted her arms, and fell back against the tub with a slight splash when she looked at them. What she was looking back, in the murky, lightless haze, wasn't the slightly loose outer flesh. She was looking at the solide baton of white underneath.

She ought to get out of the water that instant, and get the hell in front of the mirror again, and if she saw there what she was beginning to suspect — or even if she didn't — she needed to get on the phone, or call an ambulance.

Check herself in somewhere, if she needed to.

Take whatever therapy was shoved at her, so that before she knew it, she was stuffing herself and sucking down nicotine, and driving Ricky to a coronary, night after night…

…that is, once it didn't hurt so much to even think of sitting up.

It was just so much nicer to lie back, not even touching the back of the tub, but only to float, delicately, in the water.

She opened her eyes, but the little blear of light from the window was gone. So was the view of her arm, for that matter.

As if she needed to see that, at all.

This was just like her, Ricky thought. Whenever there was a problem, instead of doing anything about it, she'd avoid it, and acquire a new distraction.

A new car. A new job. A new carpet.

Like that time, months back, when he had talked about moving out, and he had come home to find a stenchy Guinea pig, its cage smelling up his side of the room.

At least his nephew had taken to it, and now the creature resided there.

It was going to be a little tougher to rehome the thing that now lived in the tub.

The little, lizard-like being bobbed in the water, flitting about its perimeter in mindless, elliptical orbits. It tapped the smooth porcelain, perhaps hoping to find something jutting and clutchable, but of course, there was nothing.

And where in holy hell had she gotten it? At this hour, in which he woke up and found himself alone except for this freakish apparition he almost stepped on as he fumbled to start a shower?

She must have gone out, to the corner store, as he knew she sometimes did, to look at some Twinkies or cupcakes or something, to try to convince herself to buy some, only to leave without buying anything.

Some kid outside the store, looking sad, holding a filthy goldfish bowl, with a sticky paper note that said, "Free." Dispatched by an angry parent who didn't give two damns that the kid has won, fair and square, this — whatever it was — in a school science project.

Ricky hoped she would come back soon; wherever she was, after getting the most ridiculous pet she could find, forgetting all about it, and leaving him with it. Not even a note on how to feed or care for the damn thing.

A note would be nice. What should he feed it? Not that there was any food left to feed it.

At least, if she had brought home a puppy, he could have given it the uneaten half of the sub in his backpack.

With a sigh, not without apprehension, he dabbed a finger on the surface of the water.

The little creature paddled over to it, tentatively, its own fingers small and fragile enough to grasp and break a man's heart.

Foliage Weekend

Where does one go in New Hampshire to get away from it all, James wondered.

He was uncharacteristically low on cash, after the purchase of his new minivan, and he needed a weekend away.

Maybe a chance to see real New England.

He had been there these many months, summer sliding into fall — and he hadn't seen it yet.

Nashua, with its smooth, long strips and signs that said, "MALL," wasn't the real New England.

If he wanted malls, he could have stayed in Berkeley. He could have stayed in Tampa, Florida, where he vacationed last winter.

"Go up north," Frankie Meyers in the cubicle next to him had said.

Frankie didn't flinch or drop his clippers when James poked his head into Frankie's cubicle and caught Frankie, bare feet on the lip of his desk, pruning back his toenails.

"You've seen pictures of New England foliage, right?" Frankie had asked, as snippets of toenail fluttered to the carpeted floor.

"Yeah, sure I have."

"That's real New England. Farms, spired churches, silly twisted roads that don't make any sense, 'cause they used to be stagecoach trails. And the leaves!"

Briefly, James had considered asking Frankie, a New Hampshire native, to go with him.

For a split second, he had a nameless, electric panic that nearly made him beg Frankie to go.

Just plain loneliness, he figured.

The loneliness of being new to an area, of coming from grad school at UC Berkeley to work in a place where half the cubicles seemed to be packed up into boxes, of feeling everyone in the place stare at you from the cubicles that were, for the moment, occupied.

So, he went, alone, in the new minivan, with no plan of action. He threw in his tent, sleeping bag, rope, can opener, and anything else that seemed remotely related to a foray into New Hampshire alone for the weekend.

He drove up Route 3, to Interstate 93, as the "Beautiful New England" road map advised, and then to an exit onto a road, Junction-Something.

Even on this well-traveled, well-paved state road, he could see that Frankie was right about all the New England stuff.

The sun was relentlessly gold. And, the leaves!

He was nowhere near anything like a dense forest yet, and the roadside trees flashed amber and scarlet.

A mauve-colored oak leaf landed on his windshield, near the driver's side window. He reached out quickly and snatched it inside, for luck, or here's to real New

England — and something more.

Here's to new beginnings.

The roadside also sparkled with road signs, letters big and childish- looking in red paint.

Weatherby's Farm. Witherspoon Farms.

And sure enough, the road got twisty and silly, unbraiding, unwinding through the countryside.

Looking at the leaves, he suddenly thought of his sister, Tammie, coloring her hair.

How she stroked it, with plastic-gloved fingers, into wilting spikes.

Then, she bent over the sink, and slathered her hair with noxious goo that made him think of the poisonous atmosphere of some remote planet.

Her hair had come out sorta blond, sorta like, well, something from a poisonous planet.

He remembered last Thanksgiving, watching Tammie's reeking, capped head as she sat in Mom's armchair, the high-backed one with the cratered seat.

Tammie had been watching one of the programs she loved, like *Hard Copy.*

The continuing search for the Green River Killer, who stalked women in Seattle and Tacoma.

And, Michael Jackson's latest —

Damn her to hell. Her and her books. Stacks and stacks of V.C. Andrews. And those true-crime books. Like the one by that woman crime writer, Ann Rule, who didn't know that her friend Ted Bundy was a notorious serial killer.

Yeah, that's fascinating, Tammie, he'd told her.

He winced at an unearthly throb in his skull, a throb

that boomed, accident, my prickly ass.

He cracked the window.

The air flooded the minivan with the scent of leaves, and damp soil.

He was approaching a little store with a filling station. A sign, huge purple letters on a piece of plywood, said, PUMPKINS AND BUNNIES IN THE BACK.

The store even had a little front porch, just like in commercials for apple juice and or grain cereal.

He thought he would stop here for gas.

Maybe even buy something New Englandy — like maple sugar candy. As a gift. For someone.

It seemed too quaint, too out of character to be anything else.

The stores in the commercials always had three white-haired men on the porch, complaining about city folk.

Or, as Tammie had called them — him — "pocket yuppies."

No such central casting-type gents here, though, just a girl, sixteenish-looking. She sat on a bench, with one leg drawn up, and her foot curled under her.

The long, blue, floral skirt of her dress spread like a fan over her lower body. Her hair fell in messy, black ringlets.

She looked up at him briefly. It was hard to tell if she was a local. She reminded him of one of those pseudo-bohemian kids who prowled the malls in Nashua, the kind with piercings on every extremity. They tromped around in combat boots.

He imagined this girl, in her blue-flowered dress, in combat boots.

In the store, he couldn't find any maple candy, or even any postcards, just a lot of standard, convenience store fare — narrow, plastic soda bottles, and obscure brands of potato chips.

This was a real, local general store, and not a place that catered to tourists streaming toward the Lakes region, or any of a dozen theme parks that freckled the New Hampshire landscape.

He slapped down five dollars for gas, and went to pump it himself.

Once outside, he saw that the girl on the porch had gotten herself an orange soda bottle, and was bent over it, sipping through a straw.

Her eyes rolled up, to look at him again, and then rolled back down to look at her soda.

That appealed to him, in an odd way. He hoped she would do it again.

She did.

He thought this would be a good time to figure out exactly where he was.

He hung up the gas nozzle and approached her, almost sheepishly.

"Pardon me. I'm trying to find my way to a good campground. I've come up from Nashua, and I guess I'm off the main road."

"Yeah, that happens," she said, stirring the straw around in the soda, which made a pleasant, gook-gook sound. "I could show you where one is," she said, uncurling her leg and setting both feet on the porch.

She was not wearing combat boots, but small, modest, narrow-toed flats. "If you take me up the road to

Wingham. The camp place is on the way to Wingham."

"Uh...yeah, sure, all right."

James looked past her, to the store. No one seemed to be looking out at all.

There was no one, really, marking this odd transaction between a dot-com cubicle guy, a true foreigner in these parts, and a slight, floral-dress girl who seemed blithely sure of herself in this exchange.

Once in the minivan, on the passenger side, the girl sat the same way she did on the porch, with a leg tucked beneath her.

She didn't put her seatbelt on, and he fretted inwardly about that, but said nothing.

She said, "There's a real cool place, about five miles, where you can see deer and stuff."

Fives miles seemed more than up the road. He stared ahead, fingers firm around the steering wheel. "What kind of stuff?"

"Just cool stuff. A brook. We used to go down there when I was little. Me and my brother."

"Yeah?" She seemed so ordinary, so cool, a native girl in her native element, and his fingers on the steering wheel were growing damp. He exhaled deeply. "You older or younger?"

"Older. He's only fourteen."

"You?"

"Eighteen," she said, with a certainty like a thunder-clap.

Okay, yeah, he thought.

After a moment, he said, "You'll probably think this is really corny, but, I came up here to see the foliage."

Then, "I bet you get a lot of people up here for that."

"Yeah, we do," she said. "When Mr. Bush was up here before, campaigning, he went to my uncle's coffee shop and said he wished he coulda come here when the leaves turn."

"I imagine he can do that whenever he wants to, now," James said.

After all, Mister Bush had lost his re-election bid in 1992. The dot com bounty was unfolding under a president who'd once just been some obscure kid from Arkansas.

If this girl had any interests, politics wasn't one of them. James was mildly indifferent to that himself.

"Yeah well anyway," she said now, "this is not a bad time to come and see it, and not a bad place, either. It's just a big clearing, not far from the road. No fancy inns around, or anything."

James nodded, and exhaled again.

For a little while, they rode in silence. Sometime during that silence, his brain seemed to puff itself out, and fill the entire, inner wall of his skull. His hands sank more deeply into the wheel, and the minivan swooned onto the road's shoulder.

He jerked the minivan back onto the lane, half-expecting to see the face of this girl, who still defied the seatbelt, against the windshield.

Instead, she only bounced forward a little bit, and then leaned back into her seat.

"You all right?" she asked. There was no hint of fear in her voice.

"Yeah," he said. "I — I thought I saw a deer on the side

of the road, looking ready to jump out in front of us."

She laughed, a "you dumb city people are all alike" kind of laugh. "Well we're near the spot anyways," she said.

His head throbbed.

The low, rumbling sound began in his head, like a distant thunder of boulders tumbling into an avalanche.

Then, he wished to God that Frankie was there, weirdness and all.

"Maybe when we get close, you can just point it out to me," he said. "Then I'll take you on over to —"

"Wingham," she said, pronouncing it, "Wing-gum. But we should stop. And I'll show you the brook."

His stomach lurched, as though it had turned to lava.

But he was not about to show this cute little yokel anything like fear.

He willed himself to remember her as she was, on the porch, with her orange soda, and her straw.

It wasn't long before she told him to pull over.

It occurred to him, then, that they hadn't passed a house for about two miles.

Not that it meant anything.

He remembered backpacking in Montana, the summer right before his college sophomore year.

So open, so quiet. He had thought himself alone until he went to a coffee shop and heard everyone in there asking about the car with the California plates, that had been parked out on a lonely ridge.

"Hey, stop now," she commanded. "Or you'll miss it."

He pulled the minivan with a hard jerk onto the shoulder of the road.

"Well, what do you think?

He got out, and came around the front of the mini-van, to her side.

It took her a moment to see her. Fleet of foot she was, in her narrow, flat shoes.

Gook-gook. The sound of the straw, musical, it was.

She was standing, almost sprite-like, in the middle of a rough circle of a clearing that was hemmed with maple trees.

The floor of the clearing was spongy beneath his feet, thick with ground cover and dust heavily with brilliant, golden leaves.

The trees were crowding out the sunlight, but the leaves mottled the ground with a light of their own.

It was quiet and serene. But his stomach was crawling up into his throat.

Maybe if he got out of there — they had to be close enough to Winville, or Wingwood or whatever her destination was, that she could get her lovely blue-dress self out on the road and thumb the rest of the way, or just walk.

Fuck you James Archer, you fucking fuck up, the crashing boulders in his brain howled.

He closed his eyes.

Then he opened them.

A steely resoluteness was coming to him, filling him, holding him steady.

He had made a pact. It was the only way to still the avalanche, and that was to stand tall, against it.

But — the doubt crept in, nonetheless. Could he do it?

Maybe it had been too damned long.

This job he'd taken, at Microcorp, was a big mistake.

It was softening him.

This minivan he bought, after ditching his ridiculous station wagon with the California plates — it was a mistake, too.

Both the job and the minivan, outward symbols of acceptability, had almost made him lose touch.

Because she didn't even look scared.

Standing in her circle of leaves, like a fairy princess, she took a small step backward, but that was all.

Her eyes filled with a queer, liquid light, with a stare that said, "Mistah, if you need a doctah we can get you one in Wingummm — "

Around them both, the leaves crackled. The leaves shifted.

The leaves thrashed.

The leaves fell away.

The whole ground fluttered, as spindly branches uncurled and began to push themselves upright, throwing the leaves off them.

Except that they were not fallen branches, or even persistent saplings.

They shuttled forward, haltingly — those ones from Colorado, who supposedly vanished from a ski resort in the midst of a blizzard.

He knew because they still had on their ski jackets, though muddy, with leaves clinging to them, and then dropping.

The ones from Montana. This he knew because they were still wearing those almost-matching flannel shirts, though hanging very loosely now.

One had given him directions.

One had let him use her phone when he had a flat — and had called him a useless college boy who couldn't put on a spare tire.

The others — well, by the looks of things, they must have come from Florida. In the acrid bog, there had been plenty of things to make short, sure work of them.

And, still.

They were here.

For one obscene moment, they reminded him of a gaggle of preteen girls, all crashed haphazardly on a living room floor, after a slumber party's night of stories and giggles and eruptions of drama.

A slumber party whose night had passed, and now it was time to get up, painfully and near-arthritically, and take turns, calling their parents for rides home.

His sister Tammie had had enough of them, for him to know.

Tammie...and her colored hair...and her goddamned true-crime shows and books...

Was she here, too, among them...these slumber party sisters, now awakening, their frames much reduced, and covered with the segmented denizens of a forest floor, that the forest uses to clean itself, and start over.

James distantly heard a ridiculous, canary-like sound.

He saw the girl, his tour guide, taking another step backward, her mouth feebly shaping itself around the words of a nursery rhyme.

She smiled, a fractured smile, and staggered back toward the road.

Again, his brain slammed against the roof of his skull, as if trying to free itself from all it was commanded to register through sight, sound, and surely, smell.

The mind that had once given him the wherewithal to bring them to this condition now took hold of him once more.

"You're all so fucking disgusting. Imagine. You used to be hot, ladies. Quite the pageant, actually. I thought so. And if you don't just go back to the slime pools you came from, where I left you —"

"You'll what?" someone asked with just the lightest of southern drawls.

The voices perhaps just came from within him — maybe from his own stammering, cerebral cavity.

But, no such luck.

The trees began to spin almost drunkenly, around him. Leaves danced, swirled, and fell.

The trees seemed to gyrate, as though trying to free themselves from their own roots.

"She sure was scared." Cathy. Cathy Someone. He never learned her name, because that wasn't the point. "Did you see her run?"

"'Course she was scared, genius." That was Shalel. How could such a withered scrap of being still possess a sharp tongue.

Cathy and Shalel had first met James Archer when he picked them up, one, and then the other, on the Seattle-Tacoma strip, one what was euphemistically called a "stroll."

Their voices now clashed, like the rasp of the leaves, growing raucous in the stirring.

And that's all it is, he willed himself to think. Just stupid leaves, stupid wind stirring shadows of these stupid broads —

Shalel: "I am real glad we decided on this place."

"I still think it could have been any place." Rita, the short-order cook, from the diner in St. Petersburg, with her boring story of how hard it was for a woman to work her way from waitress to the male-dominated world of short-order cooks.

But most of them, now, shuffling, sighing, limbs snapping, agreed — this place made sense.

This place mattered.

This place, glittering with the fire hues of New England in fall, the sheltering circle within the woods, was so much more than merely a good lure.

James, the consummate lurer, would have known that.

Maybe he sensed it. The nameless fears that dogged him here, made cruel sense now.

And, this, too — they wanted it to be a special place, for a special rite, a special passage.

A ceremony. A rite of divorce.

Divorcing him from them.

Cathy: "Anyone feel guilty about using her?"

"A little," someone admitted. Anna. Anna, snapped right off the bright, California college campus.

The lie they had fed her, in her dream, about her and her brother coming here, as kids.

It had seemed so easy, breathing that story into her ear, getting her to walk the short path from her house to that store.

Wingham, a town she'd never even stepped foot in.

"I used to think no one could make me do anything," Cathy sighed.

"We all thought that." Sharon, disquieted, at last.

They had come for him, not with knives, or guns, or hammers, but with the flurry of their own bones, and a plan they agreed was not the best of plans, but it had worked, all the same.

Bones that had hobbled, guided by this plan, guided by a nameless reckoning.

But, here now after this long journey, this agonizing awakening, they worked to their purpose.

Splinters of ribs flew to his eyes.

Femurs forced out the backs of his knees, forcing him to fall to the ground.

There, they set to their real task.

With their mandibles, with chipped, lower rows of teeth, they labored to free the cargo of James' cranium, now so brittle with shock from all it had sensed, taken in, processed, and failed to dismiss.

Anna: "I don't think he is ever going to nurse another idea."

They laughed. Their laughter, like their words, was carried within their frail vessels, but the cool autumn breeze gave it volume.

James' mouth pooled with silvery spittle.

He might have already passed from shock, but that will that had driven him to every dreadful destination, up to now, worked against him in this final course.

Words would not come forth, because the route of transit was gone — from the higher functions of neural intricacy, to the mouth that had once conveyed them with such deceptive clarity.

The moon, its grave light shifting through the clearing, through a shimmer of white across all that remained.

The leaves and the twigs snapped and gasped with the approach of an unleashed dog.

Moon and puzzlement filled the eyes of the dog, which pulled back its forepaw with a whine and shudder.

There was no other sound — except the autumn wind, once again, ticking at leaves remaining on the branches, and ushering them from their high places.

Kites

Uzamnica. Bosnia and Herzegovina, August, 1992.

Merjern is the first to try something. I am not surprised.

At night, she slips out of her bed and pokes me, until I turn my head toward her.

I haven't been sleeping, just pretending, because I don't really want to deal with her or any of the others. But it's no use. She knows I cannot possibly be asleep.

In the guard tower's chalky light that comes through the translucent, dirt-smeared window, she holds up what at first looks like a very wet and thin rag, the kind you could use to polish furniture.

But as my eyes adjust to the murky light, I see that the fabric has no weave.

She sees my puzzlement, and so she pulls up her skirt, almost to her breasts. There, in the soft plume of her belly, is nothing but the dark and gleaming underneath.

For all my pain — and always, I have pain — I bolt up in bed. "What's the matter with you?" I hiss at her. "I didn't even hear you do it!" Not a sound. Not a scream.

Not even a whimper.

"Esma, I have no more screams to make," she says, with a matter-of-fact sigh.

I cannot argue with her. We did enough screaming, I am very certain, when we first came here, and were in the other room. Now, there is no reason to scream. Nothing will come of it.

"Actually, Esma, I have only started," Merjern says. "I wanted to see if I could do it."

"So, that's why you are doing this?" I hissed back at her. "To prove you can't feel pain?"

"No, I am doing it because there is nothing else to do." Her face wears an almost-silly grin, and honestly, at such a time, it's a little infuriating. "I am tired of waiting. And besides, I have not had a shower these many weeks. I can hardly stand to lie in my own filthy skin."

It's not the lack of washing that makes her or any of us feel filthy. It doesn't need saying aloud, so I don't.

It's clear she is past any kind of discussion of what she has done. But, knowing her as long as I have, I feel I should try. "You'll only make things worse for yourself. If they catch you hurting yourself like this, you are sure to get worse."

Now, it looks as if it's her turn to grow infuriated — a searing heat in her eyes, even in the poor light, as if she wants to claw at my face.

"I have had the worst," she pronounces, as if this is true only for herself, and not every woman in this compound. "I want to feel clean. I want to grow a whole new skin. Without a blemish. Without — without a history." Tears glint in those fierce eyes. "And I have to start somewhere."

I roll my eyes a little — pain is wincing all through me — and I lie back down. I am wondering how she did this, since no one here has anything so simple as a nail filer, or anything that could be fashioned into an implement of self-mutilation.

Even the windows are not really glass, but some kind of plastic, and they cannot be broken. Besides, they are so high up, no one can reach them.

"It's easy," she says, as if she's read my thoughts.

Am I that exposed, that torn now, that even my thoughts are prone?

She holds up her hand. I see her long, spade-shaped fingernails, and can see the shadows of dark film just underneath their beveled tips.

"Men don't think of these things," she says. She has chewed them meticulously into shape.

Then, with unexpected softness — a softness I had thought dead in this place — she says, "Thank you for indulging me, Esma. I had to tell someone. Please excuse me."

But I've had enough. It's like her display is one more act of filth, of violation.

"Get the hell out of here," I hiss at her. But as she turns her back to me, and drifts toward her own bed, to continue her newfound craft unabated, I feel something a little like admiration.

To rest now is impossible. Before she disturbed me, I didn't hear a thing. Some of us lie awake and gasp, or sit upright sharply with every little sound. But not me.

Not anymore. From early on, I grew fond of just staring at the ceiling, and studying its blankness, imagining myself as a little girl, running through the meadow behind my house, and flying my homemade kites.

After Merjern's exhibition, I try desperately to erase her image, her display, and recreate in my mind, the meadow, and the kites. I cannot. Every shudder, every sigh, every slide of the sheets, makes me imagine Merjern's hands, her purposefully-styled nails, at their hideous work.

What she is doing is stupid, of course, and a bit after the fact. She should have thought to flay herself before and make herself completely repulsive to those men who came into the first room we were in when we arrived here.

I don't remember what it looked like. I only remember the shrieks ricocheting from wall to wall, and tromping of boots. Oh, and the pain, of course, I remember, and still carry, the pain.

When I can't lie back and imagine my meadow and my kites, the pain hugs me with every breath, and with every twitch in my legs and belly.

Just think, we were relieved when they led us out of there, to this place, where we are brought food, but otherwise unacknowledged, and untouched.

We even have a promise that the release date will be, well...soon. Just, not too soon.

But it didn't take any sort of genius to realize why we are here, and why a release date was to be slated, but not until a certain time.

I understood all this the first morning I woke up, and purged what felt like the entire world out of my stomach, and I felt the twinge of something other than my own self against the wall of my belly.

Very simply, they are keeping us here, with unbreakable windows, or sharp instruments, or even brooms or coat hangers, until it is far too late.

Says the snickering guard — not even really a guard, just a tallish boy, with a gun — who winks at one of the girls as he brings in a tray of bowls of some kind of meal: "You are all blessed among women."

Perhaps they can wait; they can wait around, and play cards, or go to work on the next round of women and girls from all the outlying villages from here to Belgrade. But, we cannot.

Certainly Merjern — who has always been a planner, a person of action — cannot.

As I lie, pondering the ceiling, I give up on my old dream of the meadow and the kite. I think of Merjern.

I want to tell her that the real thing that needs to be purged isn't on the outside.

It's within the deepest, most scarred place of all.

As if in reproach, a hard ball of new pain presses against my inside. I place my hand flatly over it, as if by doing so, I can silence it, smother it.

It is then that I take my eyes from the ceiling, and look at my hand, riding the fatty, half-moon of my abdomen. My hand, which has not held a nail file or nail clipper or even a bottle of nail polish, in what seems like forever.

The nails are long now, and with so much neglect, they have grown shovel-shaped.

Merjern is right. Men never think of these things.

Oh, they think about weapons, and objects of torture and death all the time. But certain agents of destruction, of harm, will always be off-limits to their machinations.

A man, for instance, doesn't reach for his opponent's ear. A man doesn't grow claws that could reduce the eyes to so much pulpy fruit.

But a woman does, when she can.

I place both my hands now over my belly. Perhaps it is only my mind in its trickery, but I feel a nudge within, like an ill-tempered foot, or fist.

My fingers curl, and I barely register the indentation of the nails into my skin, into the first few layers.

I feel the ripple of restless bulk, and I want to pipeline a command to it, through the cord I know is knitting, weaving, keeping it stitched to me, on the inside — stop that. Lie still.

And such a poor choice of words, even in mere thought. I had heard them enough, in my time in that other room.

The air sparkles now, with flecks of white light. I blink, as little stabs of fire from my nails find their way, not slowly, but with a little "pop," beneath.

I am entrenched now, and I know that if I am slow and meticulous, and sure, I will do the one thing I am sick of doing — waiting. My teeth grit, grinding at their edges. I squeeze my eyes shut, hard, but I cannot squeeze out the dancing white sparks of light.

Ready, ready I tell myself, and breathe out. I pull.

I open my mouth. No sound comes out.

My heart starts thrashing. That other, singular primitive, lodged deep within me, starts thrashing, too, or at least my mind tells me so.

Do I hear screams jarring the stagnant air? Perhaps.

But there is hardly time to ponder anything — not even a scream — how many, or how much, or how long.

Time — I am sick of it. It still comes, and violates me, night after night, in the absence of anything like sleep.

My hands restore themselves, this time resting over the snaky throb of muscle. A breath, a long one, followed by a breath that comes short, and sharp.

And, again, the dig.

My ears howl with the sopping tear, and my nostrils roil with the scorching, thunderous stench.

I have become like Vesuvius, bubbling, spitting up my molten core of blood.

The air roars around me. I grind my teeth, and I dig, and pull.

It's a progression that becomes startlingly easier, as I acclimate more with each dig, each layer, until the glowing curve of my dark, inner vessel gleams like a polished, irregular vase.

It rocks with the twisting and gnashing of panic within it.

My heart throws itself, again and again into my ribs, as if trying to release itself, as I am trying to release myself with my only weapons, my own hands.

I breathe with a forceful greed now, as if I am the only one in the room who needs air.

I clench and I pull, like some possessed potter, gauging at bobbing clay on a wheel.

There it is now, before me — the blear of the half-transparent bag of membrane. Within it, the secret —

but not lying peacefully; rather, contracting in on itself, like a caterpillar in a cocoon, trying to hide within its own body.

With the snag of one nail, I give the release, and a searing tide splashes over me.

I scream, and it's for real, this time, I am sure — not a mere echo in my mind — and the scream is not all my own.

Someone is screaming with me, too, but in a pitiful rage, as the soft moon of a head connects with the harsh air of the room.

It slashes at the gaping, slippery doorway of flesh, as if it can cover itself up again.

It is then that I really look at it, my eyes fighting for the sparse light to focus.

I expect to see — what, I don't know — fangs, a second head, cruelly webbed fingers, anything that is the signature of legions of fathers — I could not, did not count. I wanted out of myself, as surely as I have given exit here to this life not so long ago within me.

But there is nothing that signals a monster, or leviathan — just a splashing, twisting thing, with a face and skin the color of autumn berries, its throat hitching and gulping until it releases a sound something like a cry.

The air thickens with the cloud of warmth rising all around it.

My stomach huddles at the floor of my own throat.

Is this cloud rising only from me, like a steam vent in a volcano, or does the room now seethe with a chain of such volcanoes, and angry monsters, formed yet unformed, aroused so unwilling from beds of lava?

My hands form a kind of hammock, and an impulse strikes me — to peel the head like a radish and proceed right to the soldier-child brain.

The soldiers — not any more a soldier than just unruly overgrown school children, thrust into uniforms dug out of fathers' and grandfathers' closets.

Soldiers had duty and discipline. These had none.

What was this part of themselves they had passed on — nothing, just a pitiable squall.

And, I do not dress or undress the head; and instead, I use both hands to lift up, hold up, as if to a christening font.

It proves not so easy — and more like grasping a frog from a spring pool.

But I lift up, a bit higher still, my hands syrupy, my heart thudding hard yet somehow like a far, distant drum.

As I lift up, the bunched coil of umbilical cord follows, like a gluttonous worm.

Over the howl of my erupting heart — a terrible sound growing louder, and closer now — I laugh as the filthy light from the windows lends a sheen to this shocked, undone fruit of my womb.

Then, a true shock to my heart — my hands fall free, slipping from the middle to the tiny buttocks, which are hard as plum pits.

But, there is nothing falling away.

Instead, there is rising.

In the gray light, I see tongues of flesh blossom from its shoulders.

Beneath its armpits, skin stretches, riddle with delicate veins, like lattice or lace.

The shoulders protrude like rubbery dowels, meeting the distended, thinning skin and drawing it out, into taut webs.

So changed, it now lifts, slithers out of my reach altogether, and begins a belabored crawl upward.

The pile of spongy cord unravels and ascends in a trail, following. It is then that I feel a heavy tug, and for the first time in what seems like a century of hours, I feel real pain.

Drops spatter my face, one landing close to my eye, and one in the crease of my lips.

The sprinkle like a late-spring rain wakens me; and it is now that I see a true change.

All kicking, twisting and writhing in distress has ceased.

Instead, there is something almost dance-like, as if bedazzled by freedom, and flight.

And my mind is able to frame a true thought — is this my doing, my waking dreams, night after night, of freedom, of flying kites?

Fly, then. The words come from my mouth, firm, and sober. Fly, where you will. To your fathers. To heaven, to hell. But fly to your place, because it is not here, with me.

My hands, shaking but sure, grasp the cord and wrench it with a wet snap.

The world falls away from me — the bed, the floor beneath me, all falling with it.

But, in fact, I am rising, rising away from the bed, now mercilessly cold in a pool of liquid that once meant life.

I look up, once more, to the ceiling I yearn to reach — but there is nothing, and no one.

I glance, to the side, and with some effort, look down.

Falling, as I rise, is the gurgling swamp, that I was just a short time ago.

The cord that had stretched upward, now begins to shuffle, and fall, leaving a trail, as if from garden slugs.

My eyes adjust once more, and I see that my many kite-dreams can only give flight briefly, fleetingly. All is fallen, arms and legs like twigs blown down by a wind storm.

But, I ascend, and until fully looking down, and then the ceiling brushes the back of my head, the back of my hands.

I turn, swimming in the air, with a painless ease, guided by my hands.

My hands. I have done all this, with my hands. My hands now run over the flaking paint of the ceiling, seeking, once more, for something to grasp.

Against the ceiling, with its filth, paint, spider webs, chalky plaster — I push, and once more, dig.

And will this finally bring in the ceiling, the roof, the sky?

The release is as a child pushing aside a curtain, and I am, with the slightest of strain, through the roof, and then, above it.

The cold is like a magnificent wash, purifying, at last, and how great to feel something like pure.

And, the outside world — not so different, really, from when I last saw it — hills speckled with the lights of villages, neat white homes that had seemed so cruelly indifferent when I had first arrived here, kicking, even biting, in the arms of a gangly teen who'd once been a friend, a neighbor.

Yes. He had cut meat in a local butcher's shop. And the friendship had been drained from him, replaced with the cool of murder.

Had it been him. Or the food-bringer. Or the one who drove the bus. It might have been any or all, or none.

I looked down at the countryside, but even in the night, I could see that the countryside had, in fact, changed. It was dotted with something that looked at first like toppled bundles of firewood.

Bodies, in actuality.

Bodies. But their frank reality provides no hindrance at all to the trucks, buses, making their way, jolting, as their cargo kicks, thrashes, and bites as I once did, as we all did.

They, like us, would not give until the last.

I could distract them all. I could stop it.

Surely, they would all look up, the gun-bearers, the drivers, all of them — and see me.

And the spectacle would provide just the moment of shock, of amazement, that could allow escape.

But, they do not see. Perhaps they cannot.

Perhaps I register as nothing more than a strange bird, flying queerly, alone, at a strange hour.

I see them, and then, they begin to grow pale, and shadows cover them.

And then, I do not see them.

For endless space, and distance, I see only, a velvet

sky starting to hint light at the edges, and through a film of dust, the winking of stars.

Also from Emu Books
by Meg Smith

Pretty Green Thorns
New and Collected Poems by Meg Smith
"Time and place. Time and space. Meg Smith's poems do a lot of work, beating back time and preserving life so others can gain joy and insights and be reminded of loss."

– Paul Marion, Loom Press

Night's Island
New and Collected Poems by Meg Smith
"*Night's Island* is one of the best poetry books released this year. Smith's poetry is complex and written beautifully. Her images stay in your heart for hours."

– Gloria Mindock, editor, Červená Barva Press,
author, I Wish Francisco Franco Would Love Me

This Scarlet Dancing
New and Collected Poems by Meg Smith
"Meg Smith's *This Scarlet Dancing* is a celebration of emotions, filled with feelings and passion. As I read, I found myself thinking, 'This moves me,' over and over. Smith writes with a rare and beautiful talent."

– Jeani Rector, editor, The Horror Zine

Dear Deepest Ghost
New and Collected Poems by Meg Smith
"This gathering of Meg Smith's sublime and exceptional poetry is a garden of mysteries. The works are strange, lovely flowers comprised of words and impressions, images and moments that more than hint at the personal, yet remain beguilingly out of reach."

– Scott Thomas, author, The Sea of Ash

All books are available on Amazon
and at megsmithwriter.com.

56917705R00091